The Paradise Game

Born in 1948 at Shipley in Yorksh... ...
be undistinguished apart from bei...
an expert at word games and havi...
self-educated, but was processed b...
and the University of York where he took a first class degree in
biology. He also qualified for a B Phil in sociology at York.
He taught sociology at Reading in 1976 and re-joined the
department as a lecturer in 1977.

He has written numerous SF novels – notably the *Hooded Swan*
series which are published as Pan paperbacks. He has also written
a book of popularized science – *The Mysteries of Modern Science*
and is currently working on a historical/sociological study of
witchcraft and demonology, taken over from the late James Blish.

Previously published by
Brian Stableford in Pan Books

Halcyon Drift
Rhapsody in Black
Promised Land

Brian Stableford

The Paradise Game

Pan Books London and Sydney

Dedication:
for Barbara Carlisle

First published in Great Britain 1976 by J. M. Dent and Sons Ltd
This edition published 1978 by Pan Books Ltd,
Cavaye Place, London SW10 9PG
© Brian M. Stableford 1974
ISBN 0 330 25268 2
Printed and bound in Great Britain by
Hunt Barnard Printing Ltd, Aylesbury, Bucks

Chapter 1

In the course of my long and somewhat arduous career as a galactic parasite I have often had occasion to feel that everybody hated me. Only once, however, have I had the occasion to take particular delight in such a state of affairs. That was on Pharos.

The day we made the drop I wandered into the shanty town that the Caradoc crew had knocked together for their convenience. It was mostly slot-together plastic huts, but the foremen and the managers and organizers had more impressive edifices made of cuprocarbon in order to emphasize the difference in status. As a town, it was a distinctly sloppy job, but no doubt they would get around to turning it into a pathetic imitation of civilized suburbia in due course. The spacefield, of course, was the number one priority, and that was where all the attention was being lavished at the present time.

I strolled around the streets, getting my feet muddy, with no particular purpose in mind, for half an hour or so, simply taking inward note of the layout. The important part—the stores, the bars, and the nerve center of the operation—was in a crescent to the north, with the social focuses at one end, the administrative buildings at the other, and the commercial element in the middle. Facing the concave arc of the crescent was a solitary hut above whose door someone had scrawled the words NEW ROME. The hut had presumably been supplied and sited by Caradoc, which would also have flown the representative of justice in from the nearest outpost of official law and order. Caradoc had a thriving private police force, naturally enough, which would be much better accommodated in the admin cluster. I didn't bother looking for it.

Feeling in the need of some sustenance after a long flight out from New Alexandria, I went into one of the bars. It was early evening, but Caradoc was taking things easy and only working one shift per day, so it was free time and the place was pretty crowded.

The moment I walked through the door I got the feeling that I was unwelcome. I can't say that every eye in the place was suddenly turned upon me, or that I managed to stop the current of conversation dead in its tracks. But I was noticed. Not only that, but I was obviously expected. Word had gone around that the *Hooded Swan* had downed and the pilot of the *Hooded Swan* was very well known to the Caradoc Company. At one time, I had been a standing joke, thanks to Axel Cyran's mean streak and a small matter of a large salvage fee. But the matter of the *Lost Star* and four Caradoc ships that went bang had turned that particular joke sick and sour in no time at all.

—How does it feel to be popular? asked the wind.

Don't you know? I countered.

I walked up to the bar, feeling unpopular but cocksure, and asked for something that I could watch being poured out of a branded bottle. It's not that I suspected the barman of harboring any evil intentions toward me, simply that I didn't want Caradoc's home-brew.

I gave the man a note, made sure he didn't shortchange me, and then I turned around slowly to survey the motley contents of the room, like they always do in Western films. Some of them were still looking at me, but most of them had apparently decided to ignore me. It was the safest course. I smiled nastily at all and sundry.

This job, I said to the wind, I think I am going to like.

—Bastard, said the wind, with implied disgust at the attitude I was taking. Besides, he added, it's not your job. You're only along for the ride this time.

I was only along for the ride on Rhapsody as well, I reminded him. But I sort of got involved.

—Well, if you sort of get involved here, said the wind, you could be in trouble. I imagine this lot is boiling with rage about Charlot's being sent in to sort out their nasty little mess, without you interfering as well.

We're being paid to interfere, I pointed out.

—Charlot is being paid to interfere, he corrected me. Strictly speaking, the Library is being paid to interfere. You only fly the ship.

Want a bet? I asked him. Charlot's going to need a lot of help sorting this lot out. He's brought Eve with him to monitor, and he's bound to co-opt Nick as an errand boy. He'll find something for me to do. He won't want me sitting around all day while he's paying exorbitant sums for my services. I'm an expert on alien environments, remember.

—Just because you've spent most of your life grubbing about in them doesn't make you an expert.

It sure as hell beats education, I told him.

Which was, of course, true. Nothing teaches you aliens better than trying to make a living off them. I hadn't got Lapthorn's touch by any means—Lapthorn had the empathy, he could play it all by ear—but I got by. Low cunning, I guess, and a calculating mind.

I was in fairly high spirits, because this particular job really appealed to me. Not just because it gave me a chance to stroll around Caradoc property kicking Caradoc cats in the knowledge that nobody dared call me any dirty names, but because it seemed like a sound, safe, time-consuming mission. Anything which made the time go by was all right by me. Every day brought me nearer to the time when I'd be my own master again.

Pharos hadn't been on Titus Charlot's agenda, of course —it was just one of those things which tend to crop up now and again. One of the penalties of being one of the most respected and responsible men in the galaxy. Even if he was mad.

In actual fact, it struck me as a slightly dumb move on the part of New Alexandria to stick Charlot with the job of arbitrating in a dispute which involved the Caradoc Company, after the coup he brought off at its expense in the Halcyon Drift, which was less than a year ago. But God and the Librarians—particularly the latter—move in mysterious ways. Maybe New Alexandria had good reason for riling Caradoc.

What had happened on Pharos was that Caradoc had adopted it as part of its big Paradise drive. Its initial survey teams, for one reason and another, had somehow overlooked a few million indigenes, and when the natives wandered out of the forest to watch the Caradoc bulldozers clearing ground, Caradoc had been strangely remiss about amending its official claims. Word finally filtered out despite the publicity blanket, and volunteers from a self-appointed protection agency called *Aegis* had suddenly started making a big song and dance about it. By the time they flew in a team of investigators and agitators, however, Caradoc had produced what it claimed was an agreement with the natives swearing eternal harmony with Caradoc and all its works. Allegations and counter-allegations soon buried the processes of New Rome in red tape, and New Rome had called in New Alexandria to arbitrate in the dispute. The Library sent Charlot, who was, of course, its number one expert on alien/human understanding. Caradoc's operations were, in the meantime, severely restricted. So here we all were. Four or five hundred Caradoc operatives—crack planet-tamers—kicking their heels and tending their machinery; a dozen assorted *Aegis* freaks stirring things; one solitary New Rome rep; plus the crew of the *Hooded Swan*. All very cozy. And could there be a nicer place to sort it all out than Paradise?

From where I was standing, of course, it didn't look at all like Paradise. The inside of a bar is a long way away from anybody's idea of Paradise, except for a few unrehabilitated juicies. I admit to being prejudiced against Caradoc, but I'd far rather have seen anyone else but it in charge of the Paradise racket, if there had to be a Paradise racket in the first place. And I guess there had. It's one of the facts of life.

There was a game of cards going on in one corner of the room, and I wandered over to get a look at it. After all, I was going to have to do something to keep me sane while I was here. As I moved, I drew attention to myself again. People looked to see where I was going and why. I'd never known so many people interested in my movements since some comedian had looted a church on Jimsun, and Lapthorn and I were the number one suspects. (They did eventually catch up with the real culprits.)

As I said, the room was crowded, but the way before me cleared as I crossed the room. I never had to say "excuse me" once. It's nice when people show you a little consideration, even if you do feel called upon to suspect their motives.

I kibitzed for a while, holding my half-empty glass in my hand without bothering to sip it to the dregs. Nobody was going to offer to buy me another one, and it was expensive stuff. Caradoc made its employees pay for their vices.

They were playing Doc Pepper, which was a good sign, because Doc Pepper is a game with a reasonable modicum of skill attached to it. It testified to the amount of time these boys had to spare, because usually labor camps specialize in games where the money moves faster and the rules are simpler. Company men like to gamble rather than play games, unless they have enough time on their hands that betting pure and simple becomes a bit of a drag, in which case the purists among them will always turn to something with more bark than bite.

They seemed to be pretty orthodox players, which was a pity. It's always easier to take money off people who believe in luck. They didn't offer to let me join in. They didn't even make a nasty comment about kibitzers. They just carried on, looking up at me occasionally with passive expressions.

My eyes wandered toward the door. It was ajar, and there was a face peeping through it. It was pretty dark outside by now, and the face was just a blur. At first I thought it was a woman—a company whore—but then I realized that it was just a little bit too gray. It was an alien. A native. I didn't know much about the natives except that they were humanoid, curious, gullible, and all female. Judging by the silence which fell as other people began to notice the strange presence and eyes fixed them-

selves upon the crack, none of the Caradoc men knew
much more. Somebody leaned over and pushed the door
open gently. The native stared in with obvious curiosity.
The Caradoc crew stared back, with equally obvious cu-
riosty. I'd thought my entrance was a good one, but it
paled into insignificance alongside this new encounter.

"Come on in," called somebody from the far corner, in
a tone of heavily sarcastic welcome. The silence dissolved.

"Step right this way."

"What'll you have?"

"Wipe your feet."

The last remark brought forth a laugh. The laugh died
as the alien moved forward slowly, coming into the full
glare of the electric lights.

Her skin was covered in light gray fur. Her face reminded me of an owl, with huge, large-lidded eyes. The
eyelids moved slowly up and down, so that one moment
the whole of the eyes were exposed, the next only a half
or three-quarters. She had a sort of mane of lighter fur
or hair descending down her back from the crown of her
head, starting off in between her small, pointed ears. Her
arms were thin and short, and she walked with her legs
permanently crooked. She was naked, but thick hair covered her loins.

The man who'd pushed the door open now closed it
behind her. He didn't have to move in front of it. The gesture was sufficient. She didn't look back. She just carried
on looking at the people in the room. I could sense their
trying to decide what attitude to adopt. What was company policy? Did my presence make any difference? It
was obvious that we were dealing with an unprecedented
situation.

There were more than forty people in the room. In
forty people, there just had to be one. Usually, there
are more. And I knew full well that when the son-of-a-
bitch who was going to try something showed up, it was
going to have to be me who sided with the alien. Under
different circumstances, the company men would probably
have kept their own house in order, unless what the
Aegis people kept screaming about atrocities had some

truth in it, which seemed unlikely to me. But with me there it was all different. I was the outsider, the interfering bastard. They were bound to leave it to me to interfere. They wanted to watch me in action. A bit of good, old-fashioned conflict.

It sure beat Doc Pepper.

For a few moments, the room was preternaturally silent and motionless. Then the self-appointed Caradoc champion stepped out into the limelight. He was built like a bear, but he had a face like a pig. For all I knew he might have an I.Q. in the one-eighties, but he looked every inch a cretin, and I could figure how much he suffered for that. He was a hater. He hated me, and he hated the native—probably all natives, of whatever kind.

He stood up and he put his right foot up onto his chair, and he leaned on his knee.

"Come into town to have a look at us, have you?" he said. It was carefully phrased. He knew full well *she* didn't understand. He was talking at me.

She turned slightly to stare at him. That was understandable, as he was the only thing that was obviously happening. She stood quite still, apparently completely relaxed. Not the slightest sign of fear.

"I tell you what, honey," he said, his voice slow and measured, with an edge like a knife "You come upstairs with me, and I'll *really* show you something." As the sentence progressed he began to spit the words out. He was drunk enough to tell himself that he should go ahead and lose control, but he was drunk enough to know exactly what he was doing. He stepped forward from his chair, and walked up to the alien. He put out his hand, and he said: "My name's *Varly.*"

And she reached out, and took his hand in hers. For a moment, he seemed shocked, and almost recoiled in horror from the touch. But then he gripped his prejudices in both hands and squeezed her hand, not very hard.

"Step right this way," he said, with a horrible, lopsided mock-grin all over his face, which was pointed at me so that I could savor the full effect.

There wasn't much point in hesitating any further.

After all, I wasn't in any doubt. I reached out sideways and borrowed the card dealer's spare hand. I lifted it up and pressed my drink into it.

"Hold that," I said. It was just to let them all know that I was on my way. I went forward. I was very glad to see Varly drop the girl's hand as he turned toward me to present me with a head-on view of his vast, and no doubt hairy, chest. If he'd kept hold I might have had problems.

My eyes locked with Varly's, and I walked right up to him. His eyes gleamed as he poured willpower into the staring match. Then I turned away, to face the native. I took the hand that Varly had dropped, and I propelled her gently toward the door. Unostentatiously, I inserted myself between her and the big man. The guy who'd closed the door didn't move a muscle. His eyes were fixed on my face, but I didn't spare him a glance. I opened the door, and she stepped through it without a moment's hesitation.

Then she turned around, just as I dropped her hand again.

"Go home," I said, before I could stop myself because it was a silly thing to say and would spoil my big act.

She just stood there, looking at me out of her big eyes. It suddenly struck me how silly the whole thing was. I'd been through it all before, almost to the letter. Grainger, knight-errant. I shudder to think of all the advice I used to give Lapthorn about just such occasions.

I pointed in the direction that I thought would take her out of the town in the minimum possible time. She didn't move. I flapped my hand, suddenly feeling that it might not work. Finally, she began to back away. I watched her until she turned her back on me, twenty yards down the street, and then walked on, still unhurried and unworried. A couple of company men passed her on the street. They looked, but they didn't touch. I figured she'd be safe enough, and I turned back inside.

Varly was waiting for me. He hadn't stood rooted to the spot, like an idiot. He'd come up behind me, quietly. He was breathing down my neck, waiting for me to turn around and look up into his ugly face. When I did, I was quite calm, and showed no surprise. I hadn't heard him, but I knew he was there because of the smell.

There wasn't room for me to close the door. All he had to do was push, and I'd be out in the dark street, all set up for pulverizing. He had about five inches height and a good kilo and a half in hand of me. He was big.

But first he wanted to insult me.

"Damned slug-lover," he said.

I could almost have laughed at the ineptitude of it. But it was deliberately crude and ridiculous. His idea of the etiquette of the situation was that bestial coarseness was called for rather than oratorical elegance. After all, come morning he was going to have to explain to his superiors that he was blind drunk and didn't even know what he was doing, let alone who he was doing it to.

I wished that I was near enough to the lintel to be able to lean back on it with some semblance of casualness. But my position demanded that I stand on my own two feet. I waited for him to carry on. There was more yet.

"I'm gonna kill you..." he began. There was a lot more, but I didn't bother to listen to it. Instead, I picked out his eyes with mine, and I used his abusive interlude to reinstitute the staring match I'd abandoned earlier. He finished up with some comment to the effect that "...you better protect your hands because it's them that you'll be crawlin' home on. I'm gonna break your legs."

"No you won't," I said, without moving a muscle.

The comment made him hesitate. He realized that I was staring at him, and suddenly he couldn't meet the stare. He almost hit me then, but he'd lost his stride. I think he felt a wave of genuine drunkenness then, because he seemed very uncertain. Doubt washed all over his pig-like features.

I just kept on staring, feeling fairly sure by now that he wasn't going to hit me. His fight-starting rhythm had broken down. The fake drunken stupor which—a few moments before—had been his excuse now became his refuge. With a slurred curse, he dropped his head and lurched forward. He shoved me sideways with a savage sweep of his arm that was half a punch, and staggered out into the night.

The blow sent me sideways into the lintel and I paralyzed my arm temporarily jabbing my elbow into the edge of the door, but I didn't let the pain show. After all, I had my dignity to think of.

I heard Varly's voice drifting back from the middle distance, saying "damned slugs" or something similar. I hoped fervently that he didn't run into any, though by now he would have forced himself into drunken oblivion.

Nobody said anything to me as I walked back to the Doc Pepper game. They all eased themselves back into the pattern of existence they'd been following before the alien made her entrance.

My drink was sitting on the card table. The dealer didn't look up when I retrieved it.

I looked around at the men standing nearest to me, until one actually permitted me to catch his eye. I raised my drink to him, slightly. He did likewise.

"I know when I'm not wanted," I said to him quietly, draining my glass. "But I usually stick around anyway." The latter sentence I muttered, almost under my breath, but I think he caught the implication. My exit wasn't nearly as impressive as my entrance.

It was a warm night. Naturally.

What a welcome, I commented inwardly.

—You were looking for it, said the wind. Don't kid yourself that happened to you. You were just crazy to throw your weight about. You knew they couldn't afford to start trouble.

Thanks a lot, I said. I wish I knew everything too.

Chapter 2

The stars were really beautiful, and the air tasted like...

And it just *felt* good. All of it. Nothing in particular, nothing special. I felt at home there. It was a kind of infant Earth. The night wasn't alien, not at all.

I felt as sick as a dog.

It was all so sweet and nice and sickly. It was offensive, the way that world took hold of me like that. It was an insult. I remained apart from myself even while I was busy reacting to it. I could sit back inside my skull, confident that no matter what that walk back to the spacefield made me feel, it couldn't touch me. I was above it all. I could afford to be cynical.

They built the town a fair way from the spacefield, of course. It was only a small port—nothing like the miles and miles of New York port or any of the port cities on the core worlds. Landing ships here would be like dropping footballs on a postage stamp. They had to build the town a mile or two off or no one would be able to stand the noise of the big babies—the ramrods and supply ships—maneuvering for landing.

So I had a fair walk back to the *Hooded Swan*. Long enough to get a real feel of Pharos by night.

It was easy to see why Pharos was a pawn in the Paradise Game. It was a sugary version of Earth. It was mostly ocean, and it tumbled in its orbit so that its season-cycle was so short it was virtually meaningless. The weather, so rumor had it, could get pretty fierce at times but the climate was wonderful. A few planetary engineers, a couple of botanical beauty surgeons, and a few billion dollars could turn the place into heaven in no time at all. In a galactic economy, the sheer abundance of *every-*

15

thing makes tangibles almost worthless. The *real* fortunes, the fortunes that buy and sell worlds and suns and peoples—and there *are* such fortunes, for the difference between very rich and very poor is measured in galactic terms—are not founded upon the trading of *things* but on dealing in services.

New Alexandria was the most powerful world in the galaxy, because it dealt in knowledge. New Rome was vastly powerful because it sold law (in the guise of justice). The Paradise Game was a golden stairway to galactic power because it sold ways of life. A rich man can't take his worldly wealth to the Kingdom of Heaven (so it's said), but he can use it to bring the Kingdom of Heaven to him. In this day and age, Muhammad would definitely *not* have to go to the mountain. Assuming, that is, he had money.

New Alexandria had a monopoly on its kind of power because knowledge only becomes vital when you have enough of it. New Rome had a monopoly on its kind of power almost by definition—it made the rules that gave it the monopoly. But everybody could play the Paradise Game. You just hop into your ship and you go looking. That's easy.

The tough part of the Paradise Game comes when you've found it. Then you have to use it.

Personally, I don't believe in it. I can understand it, but I don't believe in it. The recipe is a fairly simple one. Tastes vary, but not much. You don't fail to recognize Paradise when you find it. It's a world about so big, about so far from a star that could be Sol's twin sister. It's usually got a lot of ocean, a lot of vegetation, and not too much microfauna (though that can always be arranged). It has an oxygen-nitrogen atmosphere, with possibly just a hint more oxygen than Earth. It looks, in fact, like a young, unspoiled Earth. It sounds horribly unimaginative and prosaic. It is. That's why I don't believe in it. The Paradise Game panders to the lightest and most superficial of daydreams. The contents of its packages aren't worth the gaudy shadows they're wrapped up in. But the packages sell.

Do you want to buy a ticket to Paradise?

First class only.

Not for me. Sure it was beautiful. Pharos was the incarnation of that which we're all conditioned to think of as beautiful, to revere and to dream of—the unpolluted Earth. Come to Pharos and be conned by your own senses, betrayed by your own emotions. Come to Pharos and live in the perfect environment, tailored to your needs, your wants, your dreams. Come to Pharos and don't ever ask what life in Paradise is *for*. Come to Pharos and die.

Like I said, I felt as sick as a dog. It was only a mood. I knew it would pass. In the morning, I might feel that it was all worthwhile. I might settle down to enjoying myself. But I knew that as long as we were here, the whole nature of the problem that Charlot was trying to sort out was going to sour my outlook on life just that important little bit.

It was a bad time for Charlot to accost me, but he was waiting for me back at the field. He intercepted me while I was heading for the *Swan* and took me aside into the "office" that Caradoc had very kindly made available to him for the duration of his stay on Pharos.

It was a three-room shack, with plastic furniture, plastic filing cabinets, and plastic fittings. It also had carpets, which signified that the Caradoc people were trying to put a brave face on the poverty of their facilities.

I was expecting the Spanish Inquisition, but he didn't even bother to ask where I'd been, let alone who I'd been upsetting. Nobody else was around, so I knew it wasn't a mass briefing session.

"I'm going to need your help," he said.

Life is full of surprises. Either this was a new exercise in humility, or a new ploy for handling errant employees.

I let him carry on.

"We're pressed for time," he said. "We've got to find out all there is to know about these aliens in a matter of days. I stand no chance on my own. You're the only other man on the planet who has any chance of reaching an understanding with them."

"What's the panic?" I asked him.

"We have to find a convincing reason for expelling Caradoc from this world, and we have to publicize that reason as widely as possible, before Caradoc decides to throw *Aegis*, Keith Just, and ourselves off the world and just get on with it."

"I thought that arbitrators were supposed to find out all the facts *before* they made their decisions," I said.

"We already know enough facts," said Charlot. "What we're dealing in now is diplomatic excuses. Caradoc has its treaty. We all know it's worthless, but Caradoc might just be prepared to overlook that and go ahead anyway. We have to come up with an excuse of our own before the Caradoc people decide to act."

"What difference does it make if they do act, if we can decide they aren't entitled to?"

Charlot made a gesture of impatience. "Caradoc is too big to push around without any effort," he said, as if it ought to be patently obvious to a child of three. "If it seizes this world there's damn all we can do about it, there's damn all New Rome can do about it, and there's damn all anyone else can do about it, short of starting a war. We don't want a fight, and we don't want a precedent. We can't force Caradoc to back out, so we have to exert the only pressure we can. That's political pressure and moral pressure. We have to find a very good reason for telling Caradoc to go to hell, and we have only days to do it."

I almost winced at his tone of voice—I wished that he wouldn't talk to me like that. For a politician he was certainly an expert at putting my back up. But I couldn't really find it in my heart to be too resentful. I'd put his back up quite a bit in my time. In addition, of course, I appreciated what he was saying. I got the message. I could hardly fail to get the message after my little encounter with Varly. Charlot wanted to do what I'd done, on a somewhat larger scale. I sympathized. I was on his side. I doubted that our motives were the same, but what we wanted to see done was the same kind of justice.

"You better pray that this place isn't bugged," I told

him. "Because if Caradoc catches on to what you just said it'll be on the move right now."

He laughed shortly. He never laughed because something was funny, only because something was wrong.

"It's no secret," he said. "Caradoc must know which side of the line the ax will fall. They can't be a hundred percent certain that the decision's already been taken, but they'd be fools to think that it might eventually come out in their favor. The only friends they've got are those fools from *Aegis*."

That surprised me.

"You mean the *Aegis* people are plants?"

"Of course not. Just idealists. But their kind of opposition is a lot easier for Caradoc to deal with than ours. Caradoc's dearest wish is for this conflict to appear in the public eye as one between itself and *Aegis*. That, it can handle. We have to make it over into a conflict between Caradoc and the aliens. We have to prove that Caradoc's mode of exploitation is *ipso facto* bad. What Caradoc is hoping for is a chance to establish that its intentions are no worse than anyone else's. While *Aegis* is 'anyone else' it has a chance."

"What do you want me to do?"

"Find me something I can use. Anything."

"What kind of anything?" I wanted to know.

"Prove that it would be a disaster for the aliens to play host to Caradoc's Paradise gang. Prove that the aliens were coerced into signing that treaty. Prove that Caradoc is importing diseases that will kill off the native population. Anything. But prove it."

I thought back to that alien. Absolutely trusting. Absolutely friendly. No fear, no aggression. What did she have against Caradoc? Nothing. She just didn't know. But would it make any difference if she did?

"I'll do what I can," I promised him. "But I don't know if there's anything I can do. And to be quite honest, I just don't see how we're going to stop Caradoc anyhow. I don't see what's stopping them now."

"What's stopping them now," he said, "is not knowing how far they can go and get away with it. They don't know how much money will flow with the morality."

It was my turn to laugh.

"You can afford to be cynical," said Charlot. "You don't have a profit margin to worry about. They're gambling with more worlds than this one. It's a tough game. It's easier for you to play than for Frank Capella or his bosses. Their fortunes and their futures are tied up in this gamble. There's no way they can calculate the answers."

If in doubt, I thought, hesitate.

I stood up. "I better get some sleep," I said, "if I'm going to be working tomorrow."

He didn't make any move to follow me. Apparently, he still had some thinking to do. Planning strategy, or just plain worrying.

He didn't bother to say thank you, either.

Chapter 3

Eve shook me awake. It didn't feel as though I'd been asleep very long, but I didn't bother with useless and meaningless questions like "What time is it?" Short sleeping is all part of adjusting to local.

"Are we in a hurry?" I asked her. She seemed to be in a particularly brisk mood.

"Suddenly, you're popular," she said. "The boss wants to see you right away. Not the rest of us—just you. What did you do?"

"Nothing," I assured her.

"What didn't you do?"

I answered "Nothing" to that, too. She didn't seem particularly surprised, but I could tell that she was interested. It wasn't unknown for Charlot to deputize Nick to help him on a job, but even when he co-opted all of us en masse into his little schemes, his advice to me usually only went so far as "Stay out of trouble." Obviously, Eve didn't know about the little tête à tête Titus and I had had the night before. I wondered whether she knew what Titus had told me about the whole operation being a put-up job. As my head cleared, I realized that she almost certainly didn't. As official monitor on the mission, everything she saw or heard might later become important as an official legal record. It would hardly pay our side to prejudice our position in the record.

She had breakfast all ready for me. I practically threw it down—not, of course, because I was mad keen to get on, but because that's the least arduous way to transfer gruel from outside to in.

Titus apparently couldn't wait. He appeared in the doorway of the cabin while I was still sipping at my coffee.

He glanced at Eve, who was still sitting on the bunk waiting for me, though she ought to have had better things to do, and then he pitched in.

"I've got to go out and see the natives right away," he said. "No time to waste. Holcomb—he's the *Aegis* man—and Capella both want to pester me with their cases. Nick will look after Capella, but Holcomb might actually have something to tell us. Can you take care of him?"

"Sure," I said.

"It shouldn't take too long. A couple of hours, if you can keep him off polemics and on evidence."

"That won't be easy," I pointed out.

"You'll manage," he said, with touching confidence.

"What about me?" asked Eve.

Charlot hesitated for the barest instant. "It's going to take time making any sort of progress with the natives," he said. "There are bound to be extreme communication difficulties."

"Won't the Caradoc people have interpreters?" she asked innocently.

"Those are the communication difficulties he means," I interrupted drily. Charlot looked at me as if I were a scorpion in the bedclothes. I got the message. I was an unbiased investigator, a seeker after truth. Capella's hypothetical bugs could safely be ignored, but the delicate, shell-like ears of the monitor had to be protected. I tried to signify with a nod and a twitch of my facial muscles that I understood and would be careful.

Charlot turned back to Eve. "I think you'd better go with Grainger," he told her. "After all, Holcomb stirred up this mess—better have what he has to say on the record face first. Plenty of time to get the Caradoc angle—they won't let us miss out on it."

I was surprised (though Eve was more so) by this decision. It testified to an amazing amount of confidence on Charlot's part. He was obviously assuming that I was with him one hundred percent and my heart was with him too if he was trusting me not to say anything the monitor wouldn't want to hear, even by accident. What he said about procedure was valid enough, but I'd have expected him to tag Eve to honest, upright Captain delArco, who would *never* put a word in the wrong place, even if he knew there was a wrong place to put it, which I doubted. I figured Nick was almost certainly the fall guy—he fended off the awkward stuff while Titus and I made use of our various expertise in order to sort out the real problem.

But Titus probably had his reasons. Maybe he wanted to keep a check on me. Maybe he wanted me to keep a check on the monitor. In any case, Eve and I set out together for the nice early morning walk to Caradoc's shanty town.

"You've suddenly become very cooperative," she commented, as soon as we were out of Charlot's sight.

"Why not?" I parried. "I'm hardly risking my neck or my good name this trip."

"I thought you disapproved of all Charlot's activities, not to mention his methods, as a matter of principle."

"This isn't his activity," I said, "and it certainly isn't his methodology. I'm neutral."

"Neutral!" she said. "You hate Caradoc's guts. It hit you for twenty thousand."

"Ah," I countered, "but it's Charlot I owe the twenty thousand to, not Caradoc. I got even with Caradoc by beating it to the *Lost Star*. I don't bear grudges."

She probably knew perfectly well that I bear grudges, on average, about twice as long as the next man, but she could see that this was a sterile argument—one that *she* wasn't going to get any joy out of, anyhow—so she dropped the matter and turned to contemplation of the countryside.She hadn't been away from the field before—she and Charlot had been busy the previous night setting things up for the investigation.

She was suitably impressed, but I could see a slight guardedness about her reactions. Odd, that. It was something that never happened to her brother.

There wasn't a lot to see. The road—if you could call it a road—led across open country which was too dry to be lush with vegetation at that particular time of year. The forest was on either side of us, but it was a hundred yards away one side and twice that on the other. We would have to pass through a bit of it en route to the town, but not a particularly impressive bit. The heavy machinery which had clanked back and forth for weeks had left very visible scars.

The plant life, in this particular area, was extremely boring. There was nothing of exotic shape or texture. The colors were subtly different from the Earth-imported stock they use to seed six worlds in ten, but that probably reflected the high selectivity they applied to deciding which of Mother Earth's floral children would best adorn her colonies in space. There was, in fact, nothing alien here at all, to the untutored eye. There might be an entirely different complement of plant families, with basic differences in anatomy, physiology, and modes of reproduction, but let's face it, if you ask any spaceman what green stuff is, he'll tell you it's grass. Plants almost invariably look pretty much like plants. There's no other way for them to look. Even the purple-membraned umbrella trees in the *Zodiac*'s Promised Land had an unmistakable tree-ness. Adaptive radiation on Earth-like planets follows similar trends to adaptive radiation on Earth. The same niches exist. It would be somewhat illogical to expect any greater differences between one of Pharos' islands and North America than there are between North America and Australia. Non-Earth-like planets are different, of course, and you get a good many surprises on ones that are almost Earth-like (the occasional giant spider, for instance), but the planets that are co-opted into the Paradise Game are invariably sister planets to Mother Earth.

Eve seemed just a little disappointed by it all.

"It's pleasant," she said, "but it's hardly Paradise."

"We're on a dirt road on a dull stretch," I told her. "Paradise consists of nooks and crannies. Paradise is a personal thing, and it doesn't go much further than personal space. It doesn't have to be every inch a miracle. This is good, Paradise-bearing ore. The air makes you feel good, and when the wind blows there's a nice smell comes out of the forest. Deep in the forest is where Caradoc wants to cut out its pocket paradises. They won't be taking any bulldozers out there. They won't be using construction gangs either. They'll use specialists and artists. Hack artists, but artists of a sort."

"You talk as if it's settled already that Caradoc will get the go-ahead."

I grinned. "No," I said. "I'm talking hypothetically, I assure you. I'm just explaining the method, not relating it to this place in particular. It's far from settled yet whether Caradoc will get a license to rape this one."

There was a moment's silence. Then she said: "What about the natives?"

"What about them?"

"Wouldn't their presence devalue the world, so far as its qualifications as a Paradise planet are concerned?"

I could see what she was leading up to. Would the Caradoc people really commit genocide, if it served their ends? Well, it would be a big step even for Caradoc, if it *did* serve its ends. But . . .

"No chance," I said. "You don't quite understand the Paradise syndrome. It's an affliction of the very rich. I'm in no position to confirm this, of course, but it's rumored that the very rich tend to get very neurotic about the things that money can't buy. It doesn't matter a damn, in the final analysis, whether absolutely everything has a price or whether it hasn't. What matters is the way people think. And the way the very rich people tend to think is that the ultimate price is the one that buys freedom from money. As I say, I'm hardly in a position to confirm that psychology, but it's the psychology on which the Paradise racket is built.

"The rich man's idea of Paradise—even the civilized man's idea of Utopia—is essentially primitive. 'Back to the trees' has been an idealistic howl for centuries. Virtually all the models of perfect society and the perfect mode of existence have a sort of charming naïveté about them—they picture people living in a state of blissful innocence. The Paradise lust is a longing to backtrack through prehistory, as though there really was a Garden of Eden at the beginning of it all. Paradise is simple. It's beautiful. It's unspoiled. But it certainly isn't empty. The birds and the beasts and the serpents are all essentials, though most people would probably prefer to do without the serpents.

"But the one thing that really sets a Paradise off—the final touch—is the simple, beautiful, unspoiled, blissfully innocent proto-human race. Not real humans, because nobody could quite bring themselves to believe *that*. Humanoid aliens. The Anacaona might have been perfect for the job, if they hadn't got tangled up in a different syndrome altogether. The natives here look very good in the part. The only problem Caradoc is facing with respect to the natives is how to constrain them to that part. The problem they're facing with respect to New Rome is whether they should be *allowed* to constrain them to that part. But outside of *Aegis*'s nightmares, the only genocide which is liable to be committed by Caradoc on Pharos is against the snakes. There are people who don't approve of that, either, but there isn't a law against it."

"Don't the *Aegis* people realize that?"

"Probably."

"Then why do they make wild accusations?"

"Neurotic overkill. They want to stop Caradoc, for perfectly honest ethical reasons. But in order to do so they allow themselves to get hysterical. They throw everything they can think of, all in a good cause. It's no doubt been explained to them a thousand times that if their case is good enough, then they shouldn't need lies and propaganda to support it. But they've explained a thousand times in their turn that their honest truth tends to get drowned in a flood of lies and propaganda from the other side. It's true enough. If they don't fight fire with fire, they lose. If they do, the whole affair turns into pantomime. That's the way it goes."

"You sympathize with them, then?" she asked.

"Not particularly."

"You think they'd be better off to stick to the truth?"

I shrugged. "Up to them," I said. "I'm not a great fan of organized truth, any more than I am of organized hysteria. I guess I'm just not a fan of organization."

"So how would you stop Caradoc?"

"Me?" I said. "I'm only *so* big. I can't stop Caradoc. I just figure there's room for me in the universe as well. I don't have to like them, though." And, I added silently—so the monitor wouldn't hear me—I can give them a kick in the slats if ever the opportunity should present itself. There's no point in being a collaborator as well as a defeatist.

Eve didn't approve, though. She wasn't about to come out with any strong arguments in any direction, probably because she was hooked up to the monitor, but she definitely had opinions and her outlook wasn't nearly as negative as mine. In actual fact, she didn't have to bother about the monitor. I did, but she didn't. In using monitors, the law obviously has to screen out personal prejudices on the part of the monitor's eyes and ears. Bias on Eve's part wouldn't compromise her role as monitor at all. Bias on my part might well give Caradoc a hook to challenge my status as investigator, however.

We passed through the forest and into the township. As we came in sight of the buildings I could feel Eve getting less and less impressed by the minute. I wondered what she had expected. Things had been far more primitive on Chao Phrya. But there were allowances to be made there—the *Zodiac* mob hadn't the equipment. She obviously thought Caradoc was capable of putting on a much better show.

She'd led a sheltered life.

Chapter 4

David Holcomb was a very young man with a somewhat angelic countenance. I was willing to bet that he was a cute baby. I was also willing to bet that he'd taken a lot of stick from other kids in between then and now, and that the inside of his mind wasn't nearly as sunny as his smile.

He'd engineered this caper pretty much off his own bat, but he sure as hell hadn't been using his own money. His party numbered a dozen, half of whom were female. This was standard tactics—agents provocateurs can always stir up more heat in labor gangs if they are young and female. Sure, the company provides women, but who was ever satisfied with company rations? (And the Paradise squad was under somewhat more restriction than a normal bridgehead gang. No hunting, no polluting.)

Holcomb had one of his amateur vamps with him when Eve and I met him in the glorified box that Caradoc had kindly donated to his people as "accommodation." Her name was Trisha Melly, and she was dressed to kill. It didn't take the intelligence of an ant to work out that *Aegis* intended to explore all possible ways of attracting justice to its side. It occurred to me that there might be a hitherto unconsidered reason why Charlot had sent Eve with me rather than with Nick. Not that Eve had any personal interest in me beyond the fact that I was associated with her late brother, but she was a fully-fledged female, and guaranteed to get in the way of Trisha's technique.

"You don't know how glad I am to see you," began Holcomb.

"Oh yes I do," I said. It was at that point that he re-

28

alized that I was going to be difficult. But he hadn't been expecting any cakewalks, and his smile didn't slip.

"We're absolutely sure that Titus Charlot will see justice done in this matter," said Trisha.

"I'll bet you are," I murmured, loud enough for them to hear.

He looked at me slightly askance. I think he was realizing that I didn't fit the part. I'd told him my name, and Eve's, but I hadn't explained exactly who and what we were. I think he was expecting Charlot to have brought along a small army of Library bureaucrats.

"You're the pilot, aren't you?" he said. It wasn't that my fame was spreading—just that he'd observed the electrode pickups sewn into my neck, tastefully hidden by my hair though they were.

"That's right," I said.

"Exactly what is your employer trying to imply by sending his pilot to get our side of the case?"

"Exactly what are you trying to imply by complaining?" I countered.

"You realize, of course," he said in icy tones, "that I will want to put my case to the arbitrator personally at some later date."

"Eve's carrying the monitor," I told him. "We only want to know whether you have anything important to tell us. We know all about your group's motives and political standpoint. You're not counsel for the defense representing this world or its natives. Your importance to the inquiry is merely as witnesses. If you've witnessed anything at all, you can tell me about it. If Charlot wants to see you he'll see you. But you have no diplomatic status in this affair whatsoever. You're no more important to it than the bums digging holes out of the hillsides. OK?"

I went just a little bit beyond my brief, but I saw no point in playing games with these people. Either they could say what they had to say or they could rant and scream and make pretty points of etiquette, but if they were going to do the latter I wasn't going to hang around to listen.

Holcomb seethed for a bit, but the girl soothed him

down. Eventually, he decided to forget the false start and have another go.

"Look," he said, "we don't want to argue with you. It's us that have been crying out for this inquiry—if it hadn't been for us there wouldn't *be* an inquiry. We want to give you all the help we can."

"That's nice," I said. "I'd like to hear what sort of help you can give us. Do we really have to stay in here, though?"

Caradoc had given Holcomb and co. a single-room hut with no furniture and no facilities except a tap and a toilet. They'd brought in their own sleeping bags, but they'd been ferried in by a cargo liner, and they hadn't been able to carry anything but packsacks. The place wasn't a mess, exactly, but it wasn't very pleasant. I could think of better places to try to sort out the world's troubles.

We went for a walk outside. We covered pretty much the same territory that I had the evening before, and Holcomb pointed out the features that I'd noted for myself. His account of the goings-on was lengthy, and not a little colored by conservationist doctrine. I let him have his head for a while, because I knew full well that whatever I weaseled out of him as regarded the actual situation on Pharos would come accompanied by a torrent of cant and commentary. It was as well to get the basics out of the way to begin with so that I could pull him up later on the grounds that he was repeating himself.

He didn't have any atrocity stories for me, which was as I'd expected. What he did have was a strong line about Caradoc's covering up the whole nature of its operation. All this meant, however, was that Caradoc was not giving him one hundred percent cooperation in delving into its affairs, which didn't surprise me much. In his time on Pharos he had surmised a great deal, and discovered very little indeed. It seemed to me, in fact, that he had actually done very little in the way of trying to find things out. His role was purely that of agitator. Evidence was apparently a secondary consideration. His eventual recourse on most points at issue was what "everybody knows."

"Everybody knew" that Caradoc was cheating these aliens blind and stealing their world from them.

"Everybody knew" that Caradoc was going to make permanent changes in the planetary biosphere in order to make their Paradise islands more desirable.

"Everybody knew" that Caradoc intended to enslave the natives for the edification, glorification, amusement, and convenience of the potential clients.

"Everybody knew" that the alien culture would be obliterated in order to make the aliens conform.

"Everybody knew" that if the aliens proved intransigent they would be eradicated, and would have been already if information about them had not been leaked.

But in the end, all he really had against the Caradoc people was that he didn't like them, and that they were secretive. Neither point seemed to me to be particularly interesting from my point of view.

I asked him about the aliens.

He told us that they were completely fearless and completely trusting. Apparently they had no enemies in nature, and they had never learned to be wary of anyone or anything. They had a moderately sophisticated language, no religion, no leanings toward civilization, and—apparently—only one law: Live in peace.

"Can any of your group speak the native language?" I wanted to know.

"No," he said, "but we've all been out to the place where they're camped, and we've talked to them through the Caradoc people. They have a man named Kerman attached to the alien group as a sort of ambassador, and a communications expert called Merani. They both appear to speak the language fluently. I don't trust them, but they seemed to be doing their best to facilitate communication. They seem to have the natives pretty well conditioned to their point of view."

I ignored the last comment. "Do you know anything about ecosystematic theory?" I said.

"Yes, of course."

He had such an air of injured innocence that I presumed he was lying. But as a member of *Aegis* he must surely have a smattering of biological sense, so he probably knew as much as I did.

"Doesn't it strike you as very odd that these people have—as you put it—no natural enemies?"

"There aren't any large predators here," he said, which was a typical fool's comment.

"What about small predators?" I asked. "What about parasites? Viruses?"

"None of those."

"And that doesn't strike you as odd?"

"Well, yes it does," he said, as though he didn't understand why I was chasing the obvious. "But that only explains why the natives are so trusting, and how the Caradoc people can so easily exploit them."

"That's not an explanation," I said scornfully. "It's what needs explaining. How many planets do you know without predators or parasites? How in hell do you think these people evolved if there was never anything to put selective pressure on them? Humanoid aliens are a dime a dozen, because convergent evolution makes for similar forms under similar conditions. Yet here are aliens as humanoid as I've ever seen and you're telling me that conditions here are radically dissimilar to those everywhere else in the known galaxy. What the hell are you people *doing* here except handing out leaflets? Are you really so completely ignorant that you haven't even tried to get hold of the essentials of the situation here?"

"That's not fair," said Trisha Melly. She'd been quiet for an awful long time—she had nothing to contribute to the discussion and she appeared to have abandoned any underhanded schemes she might have had vaguely in mind. Either she'd decided I wasn't worth bothering with, being only the hired help, or she'd decided that she wasn't up to it.

"It sure as hell *is* fair," I told her, and couldn't resist adding: "I'm the guy who gets to say what's fair and what's not, remember?"

"Now look," said Holcomb. "The points you make had not actually escaped me. Certainly life on Pharos follows an odd pattern. But they're not the important points.

What's important is what Cardoc intends to do to this world and its people. Certainly these people are worth close attention, but surely we have to save them first."

I raised my eyes to the sky, as if hoping for inspiration.

"You don't even understand what's going on," I complained.

"Not at all," he countered. "I understand perfectly what's going on. Maybe not from your point of view—I'm not a New Alexandrian. I'm a humanitarian. I understand perfectly well that the Caradoc Company is about to rape this world, and I intend to do everything in my power to stop it. I'm very sorry, but I haven't got your narrow-minded scientific viewpoint."

I wasn't a New Alexandrian, but I let that pass. I also had my own ideas about who was narrow-minded, but I let that pass as well.

"Has it occurred to you," I said, "that there might be two sides to the argument? Has it occurred to you that from Caradoc's point of view it is dealing with a completely amenable people who have no objections whatsoever to what Caradoc wants to do here? Has it occurred to you that if the alien law is 'Live in Peace' they might *want* to welcome other people to your world? Has it occurred to you that you haven't got a single shred of evidence that Caradoc is acting outside the interests of the people of this world?"

"The facts," he said stubbornly, "speak for themselves."

"You don't even know what the bloody facts are!" I said. My voice was raised, and I became conscious for the first time that we were attracting a good deal of attention from other people in the streets where we were walking. Caradoc ears were hanging on every word.

"Caradoc's presence here, and its declared intent to exploit this world as a Paradise planet, are the only facts which matter. That and the fact that there is an alien race native to the world."

"If you think it's as simple as that," I said, "then you have a pretty simple mind."

"Yes it is," insisted the woman. "Everything else is just

a blind. Excuses for exploitation. We have no right here. It's not our world."

"You just dismissed centuries of history, and legal problems that a whole world is trying to unravel," I pointed out. "You're millennia out of date. Sure, we should never have left Earth. The Europeans should never have colonized America and Australia. The Pleistocenes should never have gone into the Mediterranean countries when the ice went home to the poles. But that's not the world we're living in. The problem we have to decide is what we do *now*. Galactic civilization requires galactic morality."

"You're as bad as *they* are," she said.

"Maybe so," I said, getting pretty sick of the whole exchange. "But if we can get back to somewhere near where we started, have you got anything—*anything*—to tell me which could conceivably add to our understanding of what goes on here?"

"If you really don't understand," he said, "I don't think there's anything I can do to help you." He said it as though he were pitying a lost soul.

Patronizing bastard, I muttered, though only the wind could hear me.

Holcomb and I did not part on the best of terms. In actual fact, we didn't quite part at all. I was backing off, about to make some statement to indicate that the official conversation was closed, when I was rudely interrupted.

"There's trouble," said Eve.

"What?" I said, caught out of my stride. "Where?"

"There," she said, helpfully, not pointing. I looked around, trying to see something out of the ordinary. We had ambled slowly around the streets of the town, and ended up in more or less the geometrical center, some distance away from the important sector. About a couple of hundred yards up the street was the edge of the crescent where it all happened. It looked like it was all happening now. There was a crowd gathering.

"Let's have a look," I said, and set off. I wasn't in any hurry, because I didn't see that it could possibly have anything to do with me. Eve, Holcomb, and Trisha Melly tagged along in my wake.

I knew there was a fight some time before we got there. I assumed that it was two of the Caradoc mob, or one of them and one of Holcomb's agitators. But it wasn't.

Caradoc was involved, of course. One of the workers was busy exhibiting his expertise at all-in wrestling. But his opponent wasn't one of Caradoc's or one of Holcomb's. It was one of ours—our somewhat volatile engineer, Johnny Socoro.

I didn't know what he was doing in town, and I didn't know what had provoked the fight, but after the previous night I had a pretty good idea. I increased the pace of my approach, but I didn't break into a run. I approached discreetly.

Happily, Johnny wasn't brawling with Varly. He had at least shown the good sense to pick someone more nearly his own size. But Johnny was wet nurse to a piledriver and his opponent was a planetbuster, which didn't leave the kid much of a chance.

I stopped just outside the circle of spectators. Eve bumped into me.

"Well go on," she said. "Do something."

"You have got to be joking," I told her. "If I join in, so will the rest of them. In case you hadn't noticed there are thirty of them, and they're *big*."

For a moment she just stared at me, aghast. "He'll get hurt," she said, in a small voice.

"Sure he will," I said. "It happens. You can patch him up. That should appeal to your maternal instincts." The stinging sarcasm left her even more aghast. Speechless, in fact. Which was a mercy.

I watched the fight. Johnny was losing, and pretty obviously. That was just as well, because while the other guy knew he was having an easy time, he wouldn't be disposed to get particularly nasty. In point of fact, he was playing with Johnny rather than beating him up. I knew Johnny had started it, and I knew he had been provoked. It was all part of the game. But they weren't going to do any substantial damage. They couldn't afford to let it blow up into a major incident.

"He's got a gun," whispered Eve. She meant Johnny. Johnny liked wearing guns.

"Well, he better not bloody shoot anybody with it," I said. Slight tension showed in the construction of the sentence, and I was surprised to note that I was a little more involved with what was going on than I ought to be.

Johnny went down, knocked backward by a flailing right fist with no real power in it. He tried to leap to his feet instantly, but as soon as his weight was on his heels, the Caradoc man scythed them out from under him with a kick, and Johnny went down hard on his arse. The crowd laughed, and Johnny knew full well that if he tried to get up again the same thing would happen. He moved backward on his hands and knees, but the heavy came after him, making sure that Johnny got no space at all. Finally, Johnny launched himself without bothering to get up at all. He was on his back, and it was his feet that lashed out, aimed at the company man's groin. It was an interesting move, but it had no chance. The Caradoc man grabbed one of Johnny's ankles and tried for the other, but only got his fingers barked. He hauled the foot way up into the air, actually lifting Johnny bodily from the ground. Then he dropped him on his head.

The fight was over. Johnny could lay still and be collected later. For one horrible moment I thought he was going to unclip the beamer, as he righted himself with a furious twist of his body. But he was only angry, not mad. He knew what sort of a fight he was in, and he knew it wasn't scheduled to end with someone getting burned. When he saw that the other man was standing still, he hesitated. Then, obviously out of some mistaken idea of pride, he made as if to go forward again.

I might have called out to tell him to stay where he was, but I couldn't be bothered.

It didn't matter, because the U. S. Cavalry arrived, albeit a little late.

A guy in a black police uniform came past me at a fast walk, shouldered his way through the circle of Caradoc men, and quickly took up a position between the erstwhile combatants.

At first glance, he struck me as being a very, very tired man. I couldn't blame, him. His was the hottest seat of all. Keith Just, law enforcement officer, sole representative of New Rome on Pharos. Paradise's answer to Wyatt Earp. Except he didn't have three brothers. Or a jail.

He didn't seem to know whether his arrival had stopped the fight, or whether it had stopped by itself. He glanced around, looking neither angry nor threatening, but just haggard.

He didn't say anything for a moment or two, then he fixed his baby blue eyes on Johnny and said: "Who the hell are you?"

Johnny didn't answer him, but Nick delArco appeared from somewhere, with an apparent eagerness to sort the whole affair out. With him was a fat man in a very expensive suit with a white sunhat—presumably Frank Capella, boss of the Caradoc operation.

The crowd began to do a slow fade, probably inspired more by Capella's presence than Just's. Three or four of the spectators, however, not only stayed but edged themselves into greater prominence. They were wearing uniforms too—the uniforms of Caradoc's industrial police force, known to its detractors as Caradoc's private army.

Everybody began to talk. Somebody or other wanted the Caradoc man put under arrest, unless it was only Capella putting on a show. Nick delArco was explaining to Keith Just who he was and who Johnny was while Just was still trying to figure out who to question, and Johnny was trying to tell someone or other that it wasn't his fault.

I guessed they'd get it all sorted out in due course.

I turned back to glance at Holcomb, who was waiting for me to do just that. "Caradoc doesn't want you here," he said. "They don't want arbitration. They know they're in the wrong."

"Thanks," I said. "For all the help. And kind cooperation. I think you've done a really fine job here. What we all need is more people with your galactic spirit. I'm certain that Charlot will get around to seeing you himself, if he has the odd thirty seconds to spare."

I began to walk away, without really knowing where I was going. Eve, after a moment's hesitation, decided not to use her imagination, and followed me.

"If it wasn't for me," Holcomb said to my retreating back, "you wouldn't be here at all."

"Thank *you*," I said. "Very much." I didn't bother to turn around to say it to him.

"I don't think you handled all that very well," Eve told me.

"No," I said, "I don't suppose you do."

"In fact," she said, "I don't know why Charlot is using you on this job."

"No," I said again, "I don't suppose you do."

Chapter 5

That night, we had a postmortem on the day. It wasn't a very good postmortem. It hadn't been a very good day.

Charlot was blissfully unimpressed by the whole thing. He didn't mind about Johnny starting fights with Caradoc personnel. He didn't mind about my extremely undiplomatic interview with David Holcomb. In fact, he didn't seem in the slightest bothered about the fact that the situation on Pharos was more like a circus than a fact-finding commission. Perhaps he thought it appropriate that the whole thing did resemble a circus.

I had the feeling that it could get worse yet.

Afterward, the others all went back to the ship. I stayed with Charlot, for the real discussion as to progress or the lack of it.

"I take it," I said, "that the true nature of operations here is a secret between you, me, and the bugs."

"There aren't any bugs," he said.

"You've checked?"

He nodded.

"OK," I said, "so it's only thee and me. Why? I can see the sense in keeping it off the record, but how come I'm inner circle all of a sudden but Nick's not? It doesn't seem like you, somehow."

"It's a matter of qualifications," he said. "I'd do it alone if I thought I could."

I thought it wiser not to comment on the sudden burst of humility.

"You could have brought help from New Alexandria."

"Not with your kind of experience."

This was very flattering, but not wholly surprising. The fact that I was working for Charlot at all implied that he had an unusual confidence in my abilities. Sometimes I wondered whether he knew about the wind, but there was no way that he could, so far as I could see. The wind didn't see how he could either. Personally, I had an idea that it was just Charlot's vanity—he relied very strongly on his own opinions and impressions, and if he had somehow got the idea that I was hot stuff back in the days when Lapthorn and I ran the *Javelin* around for New Alexandria, there was nothing in the galaxy would make him relinquish that notion.

"Have you got anything for me?" he asked.

"I don't know," I said. "I saw Holcomb, but I think you already knew that would be a waste of time. He's here to gratify some weird hang-up of his own. He isn't seriously interested in Pharos or the natives. I only saw one of his followers—a girl. Also struck me as being somewhat screwed-up. I thought she was going to go to work on me, but either Eve put her off or I put her off, or she decided it would be better not to bother.

"Anyway, that's all irrelevant really. Holcomb did put me on one track of thought which you've undoubtedly uncovered for yourself. He told me—obviously without realizing the inferences—that life here isn't subjected to the stresses and strains that have shaped it on other worlds. He told me that the sole native law—so far as he knows— is 'Live in Peace.' That struck me as an odd law, for various reasons, but you know that I'm cynical. It struck me that it wasn't so much a law as a description of the pattern of life here. After I left Holcomb, I set about trying to verify that. I went for a lovely walk in the Garden of Eden with Eve. She didn't understand what was going on, and I didn't explain. I think she'd probably be grateful if you let her go with someone else tomorrow.

"I examined the plants fairly closely. They all seemed moderately ordinary. I looked carefully for signs of blight or attack by insect parasites, but found nothing. What's more, I found no insects, no spiders, hardly any microfauna at all. The things I did find all look like worms, but they're not like worms on most worlds. They reminded me more of marine forms—like mobile seaweed.

"Obviously, I can't make any rational comment on the larger animal life on the basis of one stroll. But everything I did see seemed totally unworried by my approach and by my proximity. That's not unusual in itself, because the Caradoc men are banned from hunting or capturing or otherwise making enemies of the local birds and beasties, and they've had no opportunity to learn to run away.

"There are some odd shared characteristics, though. They have no teeth. None of them. I couldn't work out how any one of them got their daily sustenance. I watched them, but I never saw one of them take a nibble at a blade of grass. I considered the theory that they might all be obtaining sustenance straight from the sun, but that doesn't make sense. There's a wide range of speciation that just couldn't have happened without some form of strong selective pressure. If they're all photosynthetic, their adaptive range just wouldn't have got this far. And how could there possibly be humanoids, if the humanoid role simply doesn't exist?

"Two other suggestions might make some kind of sense. One: there might be an extremely strong selective agent that we can't see, and which might act in a way that we haven't come across before. Two: the whole damn thing might be artificial. We're out on the rim here, a long, long way from Chao Phrya. But now we know the Indris once existed, it might make sense to take another look at quite a lot of things that we thought we had off pat. We know that it could be done."

"Which of these two do you favor?" asked Charlot.

I shrugged. "Emotionally, the first. After Chao Phrya, I'm liable to be seeing Indrises everywhere I look, for a while, so I think the second idea is logically exaggerated in my mind. The first one is the better assumption, according to Occam's razor. But there are basic facts still to be decided. Perhaps you've made more progress with those. Presumably you've been having a good look at what's-his-name's findings."

"Merani," said Charlot, supplying the missing name. "Yes, I've had a brief look at them. I was more interested today in making a close inspection of his work with the natives. I think I can get a lot closer to the nature of things here through his linguistic analyses than through his scientific observations. His biologists, unfortunately, stick pretty close to the rules. They record the data, not their comments. You can't do linguistic analysis that way, so there's more actual intelligence and understanding in the work that's been done on breaking the communications barrier."

"Any sign of Anacaon-type complexities?" I asked.

He shook his head. He reached up with his hand then, and passed it over his forehead while he squeezed his eyes shut as if to try to clear a slight headache. The light in the shack was a bit on the bright side, but he'd also had a long working day. He looked suddenly old, though, and it occurred to me to wonder whether he might not be feeling the pace a bit.

"You want to jack it in and get some sleep?" I asked him.

"No," he said. "You'd better know what I've found so far. I'll cut it as short as possible. The native language is very simple. The vocabulary appears to be no more than five or six hundred words. Whole areas of reference are missing. They're all biologically female, as you know, so the sexual spectrum of the language is missing. So is the kinship spectrum. They have no idea of relationships, so far as Merani could ascertain. There are other oddities of minor significance, but the most important features of the language, so far as I can see, are that they have no generic name for themselves, and they have no word for death."

"You can't infer from that that they don't die," I said. "There are things that some people just don't talk about."

"Quite so," he said. "But it sharpened my perspective. I haven't found any evidence whatsoever, of any kind, that the concept of death exists on Pharos. It seems at least possible that things don't die here."

It was a moderately startling idea. "I'll bear it in mind," I said, unnecessarily. "This business of all being female —do you have that sorted out from a biological point of view?"

"It's fairly simple, superficially. But all we know is superficial. No dissections, no births. The language *does* contain a word which Merani has translated as 'birth,' but there's a good deal of doubt about it. There are no children in the encampment. It's possible that the label 'female' is not really applicable to these people."

"You've considered the beehive analogy, I suppose?"

"Briefly," he said. "No conclusions." He was looking tired.

"Is there anything else I ought to know?" I asked him. "I'm pretty worn out myself. The air here is nice and invigorating, but it seems to me that it's put my metabolism in a higher gear. I suppose there's no question of anything else but gruel to eat while we're here?"

I shouldn't really have added the afterthought, as I wanted to close down for the night, but it seemed important at the time.

"The Caradoc biologists have done some food tests," Charlot told me, "but their results seem to be worrying them. They've not freed anything local as edible. I'll have a close look at their results some time. Caradoc ships in some synthetics to keep the crews happy—they find it's economical in terms of morale and productivity—but they won't release any for us. As far as they're concerned we can supply ourselves. I'm sorry—if I'd considered it, I could have ordered the *Hooded Swan* supplied better.

"As to whether there's anything else . . . you're right, this is a very exhausting world. You'd better come out with me to the encampment tomorrow, and we can do some work on the various mountains of data together. You could help by keeping Kerman off my back as well."

"He giving you trouble?"

"No, he's giving me too much help. He knows nothing and having him continually on my back is a veritable plague."

"I'll do what I can," I promised.

Once I was out in the cool night air, the absurdity of the situation hit me. Here I was feeling sorry for Titus Charlot, the bane of my life. But it wasn't really so absurd. You can get used to anything—even slavery

—and I always prided myself on my realism and my ability to adapt to situations. Things could be a lot worse.

I knew the wind would approve, and he did. I would have liked to talk to him at some length about his own reactions to the Pharos puzzle, but I hadn't been lying to Charlot when I told him that I was pretty worn out. The atmosphere here *did* seem to be moving me a little faster than I was used to, as if I were on a slight high all day long.

Something about this world smells, I said.

—Smells very nice, commented the wind. He was referring to the sweet perfume which permeated the forest, and which drifted out of it on the breeze.

I was speaking figuratively, I said.

—I was trying to draw your attention to something strange, he said.

I realized immediately what he meant. Pharos did, in fact, smell very nice. Why? Plants on most worlds have scent to attract insects. Come to that, decorative flowers usually exist purely and simply to attract insects. But the plants here could hardly be insect-pollinated.

It's not that strange, I said. There are lots of animals here. Maybe the plants are animal- or bird-pollinated. They could still have scent and flowers.

—That's not the point, said the wind. Insects and birds don't pollinate plants out of altruism. They have a motive for following scents and milking flowers. It's bribery. But how would the plants on Pharos go about offering a lure? What attracts the pollinators?

I *was* tired. So tired I wasn't thinking straight.

You're right, I said to the wind. The whole thing positively reeks of sweet perfume. This world is all dressed up. It's got no apparent functional design at all.

—*That,* he said, depends on the sort of function you're looking for.

It's a Paradise, I said. It's perfect for the Paradise Game. Is that its function? A custom-designed Paradise. But custom-designed for whom? You know as well as I do that the Paradise syndrome is as absolutely specific to humanity as you can get. I keep looking for Indris but I'm sure it's not as simple as that.

—It's a trap, he said.

Charming, I came back. What a lovely idea that is. Building a planet as a human-being trap. There must be an easier way.

—I was speaking figuratively, he said.

I know, I said, I know. I only wish I didn't run to the same kind of suspicions. But this is a world which seems to be completely free of *nasty* surprises. Caradoc crews have been here months, and nothing's gone wrong with them. Or if it has they haven't told us about it.

—Maybe I've been corrupted by your nasty suspicious mind, he said.

And maybe he had at that. But it was entirely possible that our dark visions came from fatigue. I wondered idly how fatigued I might be *without* the wind's kind support. Or maybe it was just that we were struggling for enlightenment, and finding the problem completely opaque to our perception.

Ah well, I thought, as I stripped off and slid into my bunk, in seeking enlightenment, it's always as well to remember that it's always darkest before it gets even darker.

Then I went to sleep.

Chapter 6

The aliens were "camped" beside a waterfall in the forest. It wasn't a very big waterfall, but it had obviously been there a long time. It had cut a deep slit in the ridge from whose heights it fell. The cascade fell down one wall of a right-angled covert in the slipped rock, so that the watercourse was backed by a stone face and fronted by the lush forest. The stone face behind the pool was continuously washed by spray, and was innocent of any sign of life. The rock was not uniform, being streaked and pocketed with softer conglomerates which had given way far more easily to the insistent attentions of the water. In consequence, the wall was quite deeply pockmarked, and some of the pockmarks had been attacked—presumably with stone hammers and axes, and sizable caves had been made of them. These caves provided shelter—when it was needed—for the natives.

I knew that they used no fire, and that they had no enemies to be afraid of, so that the caves were only a huddling place against the cold of winter and the rain. The natives had no use for them at the present, but they had stayed by the pool. Apparently, said Charlot, they enjoyed bathing.

What struck me most forcibly about the caves in the rock face was that they were so difficult to gain access to. In order to reach them, one had to cross the pool, and the only way to do that was by swimming the pool and climbing the face. There was no ledge behind the waterfall by which the natives could take an easier route. I couldn't really see the point. If they had to get wet in order to get to their shelter, there was hardly much point to it as a refuge from the rain. Similarly, if they were

46

hardy enough to cross and recross the pool in winter—
and winter here was not very harsh—they hardly needed
a hidey-hole to keep them from the cold. The caves, like
so much about the natives, did not make sense.

Caradoc had established a small base here for the pur-
poses of studying the natives and their habitat. Obviously,
the crews had declined the opportunity to share the apparent native way of life by moving into the caves. They
had erected a small cluster of tents—some on an apron of
bare rock which fringed the pool where the watercourse
narrowed again to become a river. At this point the river
was narrow enough to be jumped by a reasonably athletic
man, but the Caradoc people had built a bridge. The rest
of the tents were on top of the ridge, and in order to
facilitate passage between the two elements of the base
they had cleared part of the steep slope on the near side
of the pool and had actually constructed a staircase to
the top of the fall.

"Why the split?" I asked Charlot.

"There was no room to pitch all the tents on either
site," said Charlot, with unassailable logic. "But the split
is fairly basic—the natural scientists are down here at
ground level, the cultural experts are up there."

"Aren't they talking to each other, or something?"

"To judge by what they've collected to date, no," he
said. "These are tailor-made specialists. Each has his narrow field of research. They compile detailed reports on
details. Not a one of them has any interest in understanding, so far as I can see—only in data assembly. It
makes sense, from the company's point of view. If there's
anything worth knowing, they want to be the first to know
it. The men on the ground aren't scientists, they're data
farmers. It's the company's executive scientists who put
the data together at their leisure and gradually assimilate
the big picture. The only executive here is Merani, who's
slow and very cautious. Whatever the key to this problem
is, *he* hasn't found it yet, and won't for a long time. I
don't suppose that bothers Caradoc much—the important
man from their point of view is the troubleshooter—
that's Kerman, of course. He's the man who's supposed

to see that everything goes the company's way. He's a dilettante—Merani's supposed to feed him the scientific angles—but's he's sharp. If he had a third of my training or your experience he might have got this thing straight in his head, and I'm not altogether sure that he hasn't. But he's young—a typical Caradoc hustler—and I think he lacks the proper subtlety of mind."

I nodded. Throughout this dissertation on the difficulties of coming to grips with the problem via Caradoc methodology we were standing beside the pool. The inhabitants of the camp were all conspicuous by their absence. There wasn't a single alien in sight, and all the Caradoc men were busy—either inside the tents or out in the field (which, being a forest, hid them fairly effectively from human gaze).

"Well," I said, "when does it all begin to happen around here?"

"The natives work to a pretty tight time schedule," he explained, his eyes wandering to the staircase as if he were expecting someone. "They disappear into the forest in the early morning, and come back when the sun's high to bathe and play."

"Where do they go?"

"Rumor has it that they go to eat. Every morning a cohort of Caradoc men go with them into the forest, the best of friends, and inside half an hour every last one of them has been slipped by every single alien. The aliens are just too quick and too agile. They don't even seem to be doing it because they're secretive. It just happens. Merani isn't even particularly concerned about it; he reckons that it's not urgent, and—like all problems—will be solved in good time."

A man—presumably the man Charlot was expecting—was coming down the stair by this time, and Charlot moved to meet him, leaving me no opportunity to follow up my questions.

The man was young, black-haired and handsome, dark-skinned and powerfully built. I deduced correctly that he was Kerman.

He greeted Charlot enthusiastically, and showed all

the signs of being glad to meet me. I assumed immediately that it was all fake, but I might have been doing the poor fellow an injustice. Pigs might also fly.

What Charlot wanted to do, obviously, was sit down with a mountain of paperwork and go steadily through it with his usual astonishing efficiency. That was exactly what Kerman didn't want him to do. Kerman wanted him to talk to people, to winkle out each and every fact from a sea of trivia and irrelevancy. All in the name of total cooperation, of course. Never an unfriendly word was spoken. I don't honestly know why Charlot took it all, but I suppose his official position bound him to some kind of protocol. I began to realize why I was so necessary to him. I could cut the red tape and get away with it. I could be rude and nasty and it wouldn't matter a bit.

Charlot set a time for us to take a break, and then we split. Charlot's dearest wish was, of course, that I could take Kerman away from him, but though we both tried we were unsuccessful here. Kerman handed me over to one of the biology team—a waspish man with bifocals called Furin. I knew that if I talked to him I would probably make him mad, and almost certainly wouldn't get anywhere, so I decided that I might as well ignore him.

I listened while he told me what was going on where, and who was doing what, said "Thank you" and just carried on. I marched up to a file full of observations on local ecology, and started at number one.

Furin said "You can't do that!" and the guy whose handiwork I was co-opting said "Leave those alone!" and I said "Shove off."

There was a quick shuffling match, and some half-voiced protests, then Furin rushed off to tell on me. I sat down with the file to wait for the result. The Heavens did not fall. I won.

So I carried on.

Instantly, I was plunged into a welter of technical language and technical procedure that rendered whatever the reports were about into ninety percent garbage. I could tell that it was going to be a tough job for one of my

slight academic leanings. I was having to do Charlot's part
of the job, and all my years of bumming around rim
worlds wasn't any replacement for a gram of his talent.

It took me half an hour to get used to the filing system,
and looked like taking me days to get used to the procedure. But I knew it was the only way I was ever going
to get to the facts. The smokescreen of esoteric formula-
tion and presentation was thin compared to the smokescreen they could throw up by talking.

By the time I went back outside to rejoin Charlot and
his harem of willing helpers, I was getting dizzy. Also
nowhere.

We sat on the edge of the apron, and I dug our lunch
out of my packsack. The coffee came in tubes and the
gruel in plastic trays. It was very uninteresting, but we
spun it out and talked in between mouthfuls. Kerman
stayed just long enough to give me a spiel about cooperation and the difficulties of working with reports and
the benefits of person-to-person communication, and I
gave him one back about not wanting to disturb hard-
working men. We weren't left to ourselves, though. Some
odd character who looked like a tea-boy hovered around
us to make sure that our every whim took as long as
possible to satisfy. Also, the natives were back, and they
came to have a look at us. They trod water a few yards
off shore, and stared at us. They didn't ask for anything
by sign or sound, they didn't try to show off, they didn't
talk about us among themselves. They just looked.

Apart from the aliens in the water, there were groups
sitting around in little circles on platforms of grass in between the nearest trees, and there were more swinging
themselves around in the trees, apparently indulging in
private gymnastics.

"They're playing," said Charlot. "But notice that their
games involve no element of competition. They don't
chase each other. They don't touch each other, except to
help. They don't even play 'catch.' The ones sitting
around in groups are playing word games. The Caradoc
people can't understand the games, but have participated
with apparent success with virtually random patterns of

words. They find it hard to know how they're doing, because nothing ever happens in the game. The aliens never laugh, and never move away to exclude the intruders."

"Why do they play at all?" I asked. "Surely games are supposed to transport real situations and real processes into a medium where they can be dealt with more effectively."

"Maybe," he said. "But to these people, games seem to be everything. Perhaps we're wrong to call it 'playing.' Perhaps this is life itself. But as far as I can see, the sole function of their language is in these games. How did they evolve a language at all, and why? It seems that they don't have any *real* need to talk to one another. Yet they do."

"Have you got far enough with the language to talk to them direct?"

"Not yet, but I suspect it won't do much good."

"Why?"

"Because there are no facilities in the language for asking questions."

That was a new one.

"How in hell did Caradoc ever get a vocabulary then?"

"The natives volunteered the information. They taught the Caradoc men to play the game. Point and demonstrate —the usual way. But no backchat. The Caradoc people had to take what they were given. They couldn't ask for more."

"They told you all this, this morning?" I asked him.

"Among other things," he said.

"What else?"

"Their survey teams have found half a dozen more 'encampments' on this island—this *is* an island, by the way, albeit a fairly big one. It's not a continental mass."

"Thanks," I said dryly. "Oddly enough, I do know where I put the ship down."

For a moment he looked startled. It was unlike him to make a mistake. "Sorry," he said.

"What about these other groups?" I said, to get on.

"They're the same as this one. There's no building on

the island, just hollowed-out caves—all in bare rock. It's the bare rock that apparently decides the dispersion of the aliens. They don't cut wood or clear vegetation at all. But what's more important is that there doesn't seem to be a single child or pregnant woman on the island, and there's no evidence to suggest that they commute from island to island, even though the archipelago is fairly tightly knit. All the data seems to suggest that the natives are immortal—the population simply does not change. And not only the natives, if my guess is correct. The whole biosphere seems to be absolutely stable—except for the damage that the Caradoc people have done, which is relatively minor. I know that I'm jumping long conclusions from short data, but we're going to have to be logically ambitious to sort this lot out. Do you have anything which disagrees with what I've said?"

I was staring out over the troubled surface of the pool, watching the natives watching me, but I'd heard every word.

"Not a thing," I said. "I'm pretty sure you're right. I don't think things do die here—not naturally, anyhow. I've found a certain amount of information to suggest that the animal forms feed only on liquids. They definitely don't photosynthesize, which was my earliest guess. If we're being logically adventurous, I'll make a new guess for you. I think they milk the vegetation. The trees and the flowers. I think they all eat nectar—every last one. I'd be prepared to lay odds that nearly every life-form on the planet is commensal or symbiotic with one or more of the others.

"I'll tell you something else as well," I went on. "What Caradoc has here isn't the ordinary pawn in the Paradise Game at all. This is Paradise, Titus—right down to the bones. It's the perfect model—the kind of primitive Earth that never really was. The unspoiled world. Eden, if you like. And I don't know about you, but that touches a spring somewhere in my cold and calculating mind. I *know* there just has to be something wrong and I keep expecting it to walk right out of the trees. Unless, of course, it has already."

By which, of course, I meant us. There were things on this world that no one could have expected to find here. The fact that it was a *real* Paradise instead of a fake meant absolutely nothing in terms of *Aegis* philosophy, of course, but it might conceivably make a hell of a difference to Caradoc. When Titus wandered in here looking for an excuse to turn Caradoc out on its collective ear, he couldn't have expected anything like this. No doubt he had good and adequate reason for expecting Caradoc to back down. The rules of the Paradise Game were all laid down, even if it did need a super-economist to use them to make predictions. But how could those expectations still apply? How could anyone estimate the commercial value of *the real thing*? What were the political —not to say the religious—implications? Who, in the political near-chaos of galactic civilization, could possibly take over responsibility for this world? More important, who had the power to take it away from Caradoc?

On the basis of what we'd found so far, it was a whole new ballgame.

All this, of course, I left unsaid. There were anxious ears all around us. But Charlot knew the way my brain was taking me, because his was surely escorting him down the same staircase to trouble.

"I think you're right," he said. "We're in much deeper water than I thought. There's something here that we haven't even got close to yet, even in our guesses. It might be something very simple, but . . ." His voice trailed away into silence.

Exactly, I thought. But. . .

Chapter 7

I spent the afternoon in pretty much the same way that I had spent the morning, and I was soon heartily sick of it. There was important information contained somewhere in the welter of paperwork, I was sure. But being sure of it only made the job of sifting carefully through endless details that much more onerous. Long before I was due for a second break I found myself unable to concentrate. Eventually, I had to salve my conscience by deciding that a little more research at ground level was called for, so that I could take a walk. As I walked over the area of clear ground separating the river from the forest, three of the natives decided to follow me. I slowed down to let them catch up, and we walked into the trees together.

I could think of no reason for their action in accompanying me. Surely they could not be curious about humans after all this time living in close proximity. It seemed as though their decision to take a walk arose out of pure and simple gregariousness.

They didn't talk—not to each other, nor to me. I remembered what Charlot said about their spontaneous demonstration of their language to the Caradoc people. Apparently, they had given that up. Why? Perhaps they thought it was no longer necessary—but why had they considered it necessary in the first place? Perhaps they had expected their teaching to have some specific result, and had been disappointed. I was tempted to try to play their own game, and begin pointing at things and naming them, and demonstrating verbs. But I could hardly imagine that the Caradoc linguists wouldn't have tried that, and I didn't suppose for a moment that the aliens could begin to make sense of our languages, which were, after all, much more complex than theirs.

For some time, in fact, I could think of no way to take advantage of the fact that the aliens were with me. I looked at them closely, but got no more out of that than I already knew. They all looked alike—so alike that the similarity was almost preternatural. The unfamiliar forms of alien beings tend to make them all alike to the unpracticed human eye, but this likeness went far beyond that. The aliens were identical.

They did not shy away from my touch—they allowed me to stroke their fur and inspect their tiny hands, but they did not try to examine me with touch—they were content to stare from their large, circular eyes. They seemed so very thoughtful that I could not help but wonder what was going on in their minds.

When I flicked my fingers in front of their eyes they blinked reflexively, but I could not seem to elicit any *conscious* reaction from them. I didn't entertain for a moment the thought of striking one, but it did occur to me to try to shock them by violating their unwritten law of existence by picking some of the brightly-colored flowers from the bushes and the creepers, and from the forest floor itself. I assembled a bunch of about seven, with moderately long stalks. They watched me, but did not show surprise. Finally, I held out the bunch, offering it to one of them. When she made no move at all, I reached out to take her hand so that I could put the flowers into her palm. She must have realized what I intended, because she finally reacted. I had barely touched her when she had gone. She just stepped back, and with bewildering speed she vanished into the green cage of the forest. The others were gone too, in the same instant.

I smelled each flower in turn. They were all scented. Then I dropped them, feeling slightly guilty for having picked them in the first place. The scent lingered strongly on my hands, and wiping them vigorously on my trousers had no noticeable effect.

I then set about following a second line of thought.

Having discovered that morning that the local fauna seemed to subsist on a diet which was exclusively liquid, I began to search for a source of supply. I could find nothing near ground level, but I had already observed the arboreal acrobatics of the natives, and I had been half-expecting that their food supply might be up in the treetops.

There was an abundance of small branches low down on the tree trunks, not to mention smaller woody plants, but there was very little that could possibly support my weight. I would have to climb the creepers.

I am not an accomplished rope-climber, and I found that a good many of the hanging fronds were either inadequately secured up above, or had insufficient tensile strength to take my weight for the length of time I required to ascend to the heights. All in all, it took me the best part of an hour to finally make my way up into the main branches of one of the trees. Once there it was an easy matter to make my way high into the crown of the forest.

I had chosen a very large tree, in the hope of being able to get up high enough to look out along the forest roof, but I found that the top of the tree was as heavily infested with accessories and hangers-on as the region close to the forest floor. The sheer profusion of the vegetation was a little strange. Virtually all the leafy material was made up of tiny leaflets in great numbers, and despite the great multiplicity of plants, the bright sunlight was not filtered out to anywhere near the extent that one might expect in a subtropical forest. The branches of the trees and the stems of the creepers were all relatively thin, and not nearly as turgid as I had expected to find them.

But I was sure that the aliens, and the rest of the local wildlife, milked these plants in some way and I was determined to find the method. I spent some time in a fruitless search for organs like teats, long after logic should have told me that a mass flow of any magnitude was impossible owing to the anatomy of the plants involved. Not until I realized that the majority of the supple strands which festooned the branches were not creepers at all, but parts of the tree, did I guess how the animals were nourished by the plants. The natives must swallow the filaments to a considerable length, so that the leafleted stem was taken into the gut. The photosynthetic surface then disgorged, in liquid form, a fraction of the produce of its photosynthesis, over a very large surface area. The natives would then reel the stems—unharmed—out of their gut and allow them to continue photosynthesizing.

But if the plants fed the animals with a substantial fraction of what they took from the sun, yet had not evolved more efficient processes for taking up solar energy, how did the trees provide their own growth and reproductive needs? And the answer, of course, was that they didn't. Another fact, which ought to have been obvious to me before, was revealed by a quick check. The flowers bore only one type of reproductive organ. Not only the animals, but also the plants, were exclusively female. Then why have flowers and nectar at all? Probably, as I had already suggested, some types of animal or bird fed on the nectar. But what did the plants get out of it?

None of it made sense. Except as somebody's dream of Paradise.

I told Charlot so when I met him again later. He did not seem impressed, nor did he seem particularly interested. He just looked tired. When we returned to the ship together we did not talk. We had already exhausted all our complaints and our bewilderment on ourselves. We were frustrated.

On the way back, as we passed through the town, we were accosted no less than three times. The first person to approach us was David Holcomb, who started off asking sweetly enough for a personal interview with Charlot so that he could explain his side of the dispute. When Charlot told him, fairly shortly, that he (Holcomb) didn't have a side in the dispute and that he was welcome to say anything he had to say to the monitor or to one of the crew members, but otherwise just stay out of the way, he began to build up a fit of righteous indignation. Charlot stopped that dead with a few well-chosen insults that were quite alien to his usual style in such matters. Holcomb then retreated, swearing blind that if he didn't get his proper hearing, New Alexandria was going to hear a great deal more about the *Aegis* movement.

The second man who stopped us was the fat man, Frank Capella. I thought when I saw him approach that he was going to say exactly the same thing that Holcomb had, and I was all prepared for vitriolic words, but he was a far better diplomat. He only wanted to help us. He wanted to assure himself that we were getting all possible cooperation from his scientific staff, to apologize for the unpleasantness concerning one of his men and one of ours, and to tell us that we only had to ask for anything we wanted. Charlot spent the whole interview nodding and grunting and generally radiating utter boredom.

Finally, Keith Just passed us by, in a carefully contrived accidental fashion, and asked how we were getting on and what possibility there might be of Charlot's reaching a decision in the relatively near future. Charlot was at least polite to Just, and when the man had passed by he commented that Just was a man who might possibly be able to give us a new perspective. He suggested that I should talk to the peace officer in the reasonably near future.

Once we were on the road again, and relatively free from the danger of interruption, I asked him what was wrong.

"You've been looking like something six weeks dead ever since the first night," I said. "I've never seen you handle people like this before. You're showing about as much diplomacy as I usually do. What's the matter?"

"The lack of diplomacy is partly calculated," he said. "We have a real job to do here, and I can't spare the time to oil all the wheels as I usually can. I've delegated as much of the liaison work as possible to Captain delArco and Miss Lapthorn purely and simply so that I can free myself for study. Possibly I should have brought a diplomatic staff out from New Alexandria, but I knew full well they'd plague me almost as much as these people would if I allowed them to. I feel more comfortable working with the people I have here. Even with you.

"But you're right in that I am ill. It was a very minor affliction before I arrived here, but the slight effect that the air here has on metabolic processes is aggravating the illness."

"Surely it's nothing incurable?" I asked, deeming the question virtually rhetorical in an age where disease—though widespread—never stands a chance against medicine.

But he replied "Yes," and he added: "Old age."

Chapter 8

I knew that something had to happen sooner or later, and it was that night that the plot sickened considerably. I was back at the ship, feeling restless, and wondering whether it was a good idea to go into town to talk to Just, or maybe to have a drink instead. Charlot had managed to seize some paperwork from Merani, and he was closeted in his cabin searching it for inspiration. Eve and Nick were in town, where they had stayed for the evening meal, and were presumably still involved in the thankless task of collecting meaningless opinions from meaningless people for their meaningless record of procedure.

Johnny and I were together in the control room. He had been on the spacefield all day, and he was looking somewhat sulky—not to say bruised—as a result of his exploits on the previous day.

"There's a couple of things you ought to check on while you're here," he told me.

"Like what?" I asked.

"I was checking some of your instruments," he said hesitantly.

"You leave my instruments alone," I said. "You know bloody well that your interest in this ship starts below this deck. You keep *out* of the cradle and away from this panel. Now what the hell do you mean by there being something I ought to know about?"

"Take a look in the hood," he advised.

I was angry. The hood is the most sacrosanct element in a pilot's paraphernalia. I would have objected to Eve's touching the hood, even though she was a pilot herself, had flown the ship, and might have to again one day. For

Johnny to play about with it was a considerable violation of principle.

"What the hell have you been doing?" I demanded, my right hand reaching for the hood, but making no attempt to swing it across and locate it.

"I was looking," he said uncomforably. "Hell, I knew I shouldn't, but I just wanted to see what things looked like—to help me to understand what goes on up here while I'm keeping the flux balanced in the belly. I wouldn't have told you, except that I think there's something odd out there."

"Why didn't you tell me before?" I demanded. "We've been sitting here for half an hour."

"Because it should be rising about now. In the east. For God's sake, *look*. You can give me the lectures later."

I located the hood. The ship's instrument panel wasn't dead, of course, but it didn't volunteer information unless it was asked. The panel was primarily for input. The hood was mostly for observation and sensory functions.

I looked to the east, expecting to see one of the planet's two tiny moons rising. But it wasn't a moon. At least Johnny hadn't walked himself into trouble for nothing. It was a ship, orbiting the world, where no ship had any right to be.

It couldn't be the Caradoc supply ship—which was the only ship legally entitled to land here while our investigation was going on—because that wouldn't hang around in orbit wasting company money.

"Well?" said Johnny, after a decent pause.

"It's a ship," I said.

"I was right," he said, sounding very relieved. "It's perhaps as well I looked."

"Damn it," I said. "You know bloody well that finding a ship doesn't justify your being where you had no right to be. I don't give a damn if you find a twenty-ton meteorite that's going to drop right on top of us, I don't want you playing with my equipment."

"But it could be important," he complained.

"Not that important," I assured him. But I was thinking hard, and the venom had drained out of my voice. I was very curious about that ship.

"Should I get the boss?" he asked.

"You can leave him alone, too," I said. "I haven't a clue why he hired you in the first place—if it was just to pry me loose from your back room I'd just as soon he hadn't bothered—but the least you can do is to keep him from regretting it. He already has one score against you for pulling idiot jailbreaks on Rhapsody. Don't give him any more."

"Hell," he said, "I only suggested telling him there was a ship in orbit."

"Yeah, well he's ill," I said, "and he doesn't want any more pieces of jigsaw dropped on his plate without knowing where they fit."

"You're very conscientious all of a sudden," he said. "I'd have thought your dearest wish was to give the old man a permanent heart attack."

"Some other time," I said, still paying only half a mind to the conversation. "At the moment he's one of my favorite people. . . . I wonder if I can pick up his beam. How long is it since he was last in the sky?"

"Not too long. Four hours plus, I guess."

"But people were busy, then. If somebody's keeping him up-to-date on what's happening down here, they'll probably be doing it right now, while they drink their after-dinner cup of tea, or smoke their after-dinner joint, or whatever."

He moved from his chair, and dared to come over to stand beside the cradle. But he kept his hands behind his back.

"You think you can tap their call beam?" he asked.

"Should be easy," I said. "Wherever the beam starts, it can't be more than a mile from here. I don't care how tight it is, they've got to allow a certain amount of spray. It's only a matter of tuning. But I'll have to open right up or I'll only get one end of the chitchat. So you keep quiet. Don't breathe too loud. And if you sneeze I'll brain you."

Gently, I began to caress the pickup on the call circuit,

trying to infiltrate the hypothetical beam link between ship and ground. I had to keep the energy low, so that if I did suddenly manage to augment their beam, I wouldn't contribute a sudden energy boost and reveal the presence of an eavesdropper.

A few tense, silent minutes passed while my fingers twiddled the dials with great delicacy.

Then we heard the voice.

"Look," it said, with an unmistakable hint of hysteria, despite its faintness, "it's too big. . . . I just can't handle it. . . . This isn't my level of responsibility. . . . I need a director out here at least. . . ."

"You *know* how far we are from base," said the other voice. "I can't *call* them, you know . . . It'll take a week to get a message through. . . ."

"I haven't *got* a week!"

"I *know* you haven't got a week. . . . That's exactly what I mean. . . . Whatever you do, it's going to be your own decision. . . . You're the man on the spot. . . . You've got the responsibility. . . . You've got the rank. . . . You've got the ship up in the sky. . . . It's *your* decision. . . ."

"I can't make decisions like this. . . . It's *not* my level. . . . I haven't got the rank necessary to handle this —not Charlot, not with what Kerman has already. . . . All I get from him—from anyone—is garbage. . . . I don't understand. . . . I can't take the responsibility if I don't know what's going on. . . . We need more experts. . . . We need a director at least. . . . There's just no way of knowing how big this thing is or even what kind of a thing it is. . . ."

"Look, will you for Christ's sake *shut up!* What the hell do you want me to do. . . ? I don't rank you. . . . I can't carry the can for you. . . . You're the man on the ground, you tell me what to do. . . . But you send me home to cry for help and they'll crucify you. . . . You know that. . . . Whether anything happens in the meantime or not, they'll do it. . . . I'm your ace in the hole, and you better not forget that. . . . You call me down or you leave me be, that's up to you. . . . But there's nothing that can make me take one ounce of the initiative. . . . It's *your* potato. . . . There's *nothing* I can do, except tell you to pull yourself together. . . . My advice to you is that you figure this world and you figure it fast, and you figure it some way that you've got something on Charlot. . . . But *get* something and make it stick. . . . It's no good moaning about experts because you got all the experts you got sitting in your lap. . . . If they can't give you anything you better get something yourself. . . . But if you knuckle under you better have a damn good reason. . . . And if you call my boys down you better have a damn good reason for that as well. . . ."

"That's what I'm trying to get across to you, you bloody fool. . . . There just aren't any damn good reasons. . . . We just don't know what we have. . . . This is an *alien world,* damn it. . . . We can't just walk in and add it up on a cash register. . . . Hell, I don't even know whether we got anything that'll sell. . . . I tell you . . ."

"You already *told* me. . . . If you told me once you told me a hundred times. . . . So what am I, Sherlock Holmes. . . ? I tell *you,* friend, you better stop telling me your damn problems and start handing me the recipe for some *action*. . . .Either that or start planning your excuses, which had better be *good*. . . . Now I don't give a bugger about you, I'm signing off. . . . And next time be sure you have something to *tell* me because I sure as hell don't want to turn my stomach over listening to your damn *problems* for the ninety-fifth time. . . . OK?"

"OK," said the first voice, sounding less OK than anyone else I'd ever heard. "OK, damn it. . . . I'll be in touch. . . . If there are any *developments*."

"That's right," said the man in the sky, *"developments. If I were you, I'd develop.* . . . And fast. . . . Good night."

I could imagine the man on the ground adding something pretty pithy to round out the happy little chat, but the circuit was out, and he had only himself for an audience.

"Well well well," I said. "We learned a lot from that."

"It was Caradoc," said Johnny. "Frank Capella."

"Clever boy," I said. "What's the name of the captain's pet monkey?"

There was a pause.

"Are you going to tell Charlot?" asked Johnny.

"I don't know," I said. I didn't. Tell him what? That Caradoc had a battleship hovering? That Capella had no more answers than we did? So what? We already knew that Capella was sitting on the hottest seat since the electric chair went nova.

"I think we can buy him," I said suddenly.

"Eh?" said Johnny, who was still thinking about Charlot.

"Capella. I think he can be bought. He doesn't care about this world. All he cares about is his position in the company. Right now, what he wants more than anything else in the world, is something to do and a reason for doing it. He hasn't got a reason for calling that ship down and thumbing his nose at the universe. He knows that's what his bosses want, and he also knows that they don't expect him to be able to provide it, even though they'll chop him if he doesn't. He's got to be ready to negotiate. He's set up like a toy duck in a shooting gallery."

"We'd better tell Charlot, then," he said. "Fast—before Capella goes and does something stupid."

I took him by the shoulder, suddenly realizing that he knew a little bit too much for comfort—my comfort—and I prepared to pull the old pals act. I'd pulled it once before, on Nick delArco, and if I could pull it on the captain, little Johnny ought to be a real pushover. I was his hero.

"Look, son," I said to him, "you may just have fallen off a Christmas tree, but I didn't. Titus Charlot isn't the only man around here with a talent for thinking up excuses. If I can buy Capella and sell him to Charlot . . ."

"So who needs you?" said Johnny, understandably. He didn't understand.

"Capella does," I said. "He doesn't know how to reach Charlot, but I do. Capella knows full well that Charlot won't save him unless he's forced. I can force him. I can force *both of them*."

For a moment, I was quite carried away. But I brought myself back down with a bump. If I was going to make something out of this, I was going to have to be very careful. I knew something about Capella that Charlot didn't, and something about Charlot that Capella didn't. Theoretically, that ought to be enough to make myself some fast capital. But I was in an extremely delicate position as regards Charlot—he'd make me suffer doubly if I crossed him after he'd trusted me and let me in on his game. In addition, I had my own interest in the way things went down here—academic and emotional—and no matter how cynical you are you can't forget an interest like that, no matter how commercial your other angles are.

For one horrible moment, I was tempted to tell Charlot everything and rely on his dubious generosity. Then I decided to hang on and think about it.

Hesitation rarely hurts.

"Wait a minute," said Johnny, who had his eyes screwed up into a pensive squint, and whose attitude toward me at that particular moment was distinctly ambiguous. "Before you go rushing off to play, there's something else I think you ought to see."

"What?" I asked.

"It's outside," he said.

"What is it?" I persisted.

"You'd better come see," he told me. "I'm not sure. It could be nothing. I didn't figure all that was said in Charlot's spiel last night. But if what he said about the way things are on this world is true, then there's something that could need explaining. Bring a flash."

"It's not that dark," I said, too taken aback by his attitude of mystery to say much else.

"I know that," he said, "but what we want to look at is down a hole. OK?"

I shrugged. "Lead on, pal," I said. "If you've found the key to the whole problem, I personally will thank you very kindly, and we can work out *together* how we are going to run the show."

I was being heavily sarcastic, of course, but I was careful not to sound aggressive about it. It had not escaped my notice that I might yet have use for Johnny's good opinion.

We went out on to the field. It was completely deserted. All the Caradoc heavy machinery was at rest—the workers had gone home for the day. All they had done while they were actually active was to drive bulldozers and diggers around a bit, idling along in pursuit of plans whose urgency was suspended. They hadn't even left a night watchman. Who would want to steal a bulldozer in Paradise?

As we crossed the field, my mind was still trying to balance possible courses of action. There was really only one question: could I get far enough ahead of Charlot to offer to sell him a solution? That was a pretty ambitious question. Charlot was a very, very clever man. He was also ill, a fraction narrow-minded, and attacking the problem from what might just prove to be the wrong direction. I had the feeling that if only Charlot, Capella, and Holcomb could get together in a bug-free environment we could work out a satisfactory agreement. Just a little cooperation all around.

"Here we are," said Johnny.

We were right out at the edge of the field. If all went Caradoc's way, the main terminal would be here, and the hole into whose depths we were staring would contain the foundations of spaceport officialdom.

I shone the flash down into the hole.

"Lousy place to dig foundations," I said. "That rock down there's all soft and crumbling. They'll have to dig deep."

"They have dug deep," said Johnny, as he scrambled down into the pit. He was right—it was a fair way down.

"Are you sure we can get out again?" I asked him.

"I did it this afternoon," he reassured me. I hoped he was right, and I followed him down.

"Here," he said, scraping at the wall of the pit with his fingertips. "Shine the light along . . . there, and . . . there. . . ."

All I could see were marks in the soft rock.

"There must have been a lot more of it," said Johnny,

"but they smashed it up with the shovel. It'll all be up there in the rubble, but I don't suppose there'll be anything identifiable. But the shovel didn't crush this bit here, you see—the face has crumbled away—the rock is very soft, like you said. This land was a lot lower once—it was probably reclaimed from the sea, very slowly. It might have been swampy once. Here, you can see what I mean just here . . . that line there, and that one. Here's the foot, and over here's the eye."

It clicked. He was showing me petrified bones. The thing in the pit was a fossil. I shone the light over the whole length of the creature, and back again. The head part wasn't too clear, but I could see what I needed to see. And the foot made it definite.

It was the fossil of an extinct animal.

With claws and teeth.

Chapter 9

We climbed out of the pit without too much difficulty, getting very dirty in the process, and began to walk slowly back to the *Hooded Swan*.

"Is it important?" asked Johnny.

"You bet your sweet life it's important," I told him. "It's so simple . . . the Paradise syndrome, of course, it misled us all. The perfect world, an innocent, unspoiled, *young* Earth. And it looked like a *real* Garden of Eden—created to order, fresh off the production line. . . .

"Only it's not fresh. It's not primitive. It's not young. It's far older than Earth. Of *course* there's evolution here. It isn't that it hasn't started—it's *stopped*. Sure, everything's been the same for a million years or more. Sure nobody and nothing dies—*now*. The evolution's *over*—it's stabilized. Something's stabilized it. Something's run the whole of life on this world into a rut and is keeping it there. Of *course* there's a selective agent—the reason we haven't found it is because it's not active. It has no selecting to do. Or it *had* none, until Caradoc . . ."

"Grainger!"

The shout came from halfway across the field. Nick delArco was running to intercept us. He'd just come back from town and he'd come in a hurry. Something had happened. Things were beginning to happen all over the place.

"You'd better get the maiden out," he said, as he arrived at a distance where he didn't have to shout. "We have to get into town quickly. I'll get Charlot. Just wants him. There's a war about to start."

"What happened?" asked Johnny.

Nick had already turned, and was heading for the

Swan. Almost unconsciously, we broke into a run to keep pace with him. He looked back over his shoulder, and said:

"One of the Caradoc men murdered a native. *Aegis* is howling for blood. The witnesses won't talk. Just's sitting with his finger over a volcano. There'll be more murder done unless Charlot can sort it out."

By the time he had finished telling us all this we were up into the belly of the ship, and Charlot was coming out to find out what all the commotion was about.

"Get the buggy out," I told Johnny, as delArco began to go through it all again. I leaned back against the bulkhead and began to wipe dirt off my hands on to my shirt.

I figured I just about had time to change my shirt.

—So much for the chance to have a quiet little talk with everybody, said the wind.

A promising diplomatic career, nipped in the bud, I commented.

—It's saved you from yourself, he said. You'd have been a cast iron certainty to botch it up.

Nonsense, I replied. With you to help me out, how could I possibly have failed?

He laughed. Laughing parasites feel very strange. It really kills a conversation.

I was appointed to drive the iron maiden—a testimony to my position as official transportation executive rather than to my skill at ground zero driving. Nick, with his long experience of groundhogging on Earth, might well have got us there a shade faster.

When I drive, I worry too much about other things on the road—like the four pedestrians who passed us, going the other way. They weren't running, and they weren't in my way, but I worried anyway. I didn't see why anyone should be going to the field at that time of night while all the action was in town. I couldn't see who they were, but I was suspicious.

"Hey," I said. "Do you think we ought to have left somebody back at the *Swan*?"

"Why?" It was Johnny who questioned me—probably

because he knew that if anyone had to go back it would be him.

"Because four shadows just passed us on their way out there."

"They can't get into the ship," Charlot assured me. "Even if they wanted to."

"We shouldn't have left her alone," I said. "We're on an alien world."

"Keep driving," said Charlot.

I shrugged my shoulders and kept driving. It was all a fuss about nothing, in all likelihood. Nobody on Pharos could possibly wish ill upon the *Hooded Swan*. The fact that there were other ships on the field, as well as a good deal of heavy equipment, didn't really seem relevant.

We found the big confrontation scene in the bar where I'd celebrated on the first night. It was far more crowded than on that occasion—they were packed in like sardines, despite the fact that the Caradoc security men were trying to transfer people from the inside to the outside at an appreciable rate.

I made the maiden's brakes howl as I brought her to a halt. It was a theatrical gesture, just to make certain that we were noticed. We all piled out as if we were the riot squad come to clean up after a brawl. Johnny was eager to see and Nick pressed forward to clear the way for Charlot. Modestly, I hung back.

We were well past the scene where everyone inside was frozen into a dramatic tableau around the remains of the deceased. The deceased had been picked up and laid out on the bar. Capella was sitting on a chair, his head in his hand, his elbow only a couple of inches away from the alien's face. He looked bored. Just was standing, and he still had his gun in his hand—which seemed to me to be a tactical error. The inner core of the crowd were all Caradoc police, except for Varly. I didn't have to ask who done it. Eve was there, too, standing behind Capella. Nobody was talking—they were waiting for the dramatis personae to be complete before they launched into impassioned defenses or whatever. There had probably been a fair amount of conversation in the crowd before we arrived, but it stopped when we invaded the scene. The only sound that we could hear as we pushed our way to the heart of the matter was the sound of betting in the poker game. It took more than murder and mayhem to stop those boys.

Charlot headed straight for Just, but I didn't want to wait for the preliminaries. I faded a few steps back into the crowd, selected the nearest guy who looked a bit responsive to intimidation, tapped him on the shoulder, and said: "What happened?"

He squinted at me. "You was in here the other night," he said. I had a nasty suspicion that it might not be an irrelevant remark.

"What happened *tonight*?" I said.

"You saw what happened the night 'fore last. Well, she came back. If you hadn't . . . well, anyways, you know . . . this time, she *let* him. . . ."

"He raped her?" I felt sick.

"It wasn't rape."

"*Here?*"

"Not here. Upstairs."

"Why'd he kill her?"

"Dunno."

"How'd they find out?"

He shrugged. "Varly come down and told us. He was drunk."

I shook my head. "A roomful of people," I said. "Cops too. And you all let him take her upstairs."

"Nobody knowed he was goin' to kill her."

I returned my attention to what was going on at the center of the crowd's attention. Someone from *Aegis*— not Holcomb—was screaming for a hearing, but he was over by the door and the Caradoc security men were trying to eject him. Neither Just nor Charlot objected to his being removed. They were trying to work out what was to be done. Just had arrested Varly, and wanted to lock him up somewhere under his personal supervision. The Caradoc leaders had no objection in principle, but they reckoned that practicality demanded their own men should look after the prisoner. They were prepared to be stubborn about it. It was easy to see why it mattered. The whole argument about Caradoc's supposed treaty implied a doubt as to legal jurisdiction. There was no argument about the law—merely as to who had jurisdiction. I could see that Charlot was on the spot. Just wanted him to stop the buck, and if he did then he would be prejudging the case. Charlot didn't want the buck passed to him.

I took one look at Capella and I knew he was working an angle. I didn't know whether he had engineered the whole thing, or whether he was just trying to take advantage of a nasty situation, but the gleam in his eyes said perfectly clearly that he thought he was on to something.

"Look, Mr. Charlot," Just was saying, "there's no way we can sort out whose law applies here. If it's the natives', then I don't see that anyone can take Varly into custody except the natives, and if what Capella says is true, the aliens don't have any notion of punitive measures. On the other hand, if it's the Law of New Rome that applies here, then we've got to decide whether it's me or them that has the power of imprisonment. They claim that if the Law of New Rome holds here, their treaty must be good, and if it is then they are the official law enforcement agency. Alternatively, they claim, they ought to hold Varly pending a demand by the local agency that he be turned over."

"That's nonsense," said Charlot. "You're the ultimate legal authority on this world so far as the Law of New Rome is concerned. And if the alien law is sovereign, then Caradoc has no claim on Varly at all."

"But I can't let him free," protested Just. "And I can't lock him up if they won't give me a place to lock him. Am I supposed to arrest Capella too?"

I could understand his problems. Just had found out that the burden of decision was an awkward one. He was in the same boat as Capella, he had to make decisions on data he didn't have. His masters weren't likely to be as unkind as Capella's, but the consequences of his decision might be far-reaching in that they might prejudice the whole outcome of this dispute. Just was as interested in this world as anybody, and he knew full well that Capella was searching high and low for an excuse to take precipitate action.

Simply stated, his problem was that he didn't dare buck Capella in case he pushed Caradoc into an action that everybody would regret, and he didn't dare not buck Capella in case he gave Capella ammunition to use in the fight for Paradise.

Charlot was a fast thinker, but I knew he wasn't fast enough to sort this one out. Not if he went through his own mental channels.

Sometimes I have brilliant ideas. Usually, I'm wary of them, because they don't always work. There was, however, no time to prevaricate in the present situation.

"Mr. Peace Officer, sir," I said, stepping right forward to make sure everybody knew who was talking. "I'd like to make a complaint against that man there"—I pointed dramatically at Varly—" and I demand that you charge him with criminal assault on me, night before last. There can be no doubt whatsoever that this crime is covered by the Law of New Rome. I further demand that you lock him up immediately in the only location on this planet which is clearly under the administration of New Rome, which is to say in the *Hooded Swan,* which is currently commissioned by New Rome."

My mock-legal language sounded terrible, but there was no doubt that I got the various bits of the message across. I'd offered Just both a safe arrest and a safe prison.

"You can't arrest a man for assault when he's just committed a murder," complained Capella, with touching loyalty to his employee. But he had no chance. Just didn't even bother to think. He knew he was being offered an out, and if it didn't work he could always blame me. He was mad keen to get out of the limelight.

"Any witnesses?" he asked me.

"Sure," I said. "The barman, the card players, and the guy with the squint."

"Right," said the lawman. "I'll investigate in the morning. In the meantime, Varly gets locked up in the *Hooded Swan*.

"I'll drive you," I said sweetly.

"Better have somebody not involved," he said. He was smiling now. "How about you?" He pointed at Johnny.

"Sure," said Johnny.

"I don't have to walk, do I?" I asked, cutting across Capella, who was trying to say something else.

"No," said Just. "You can ride in the back."

He didn't wait to hear whatever else it was that Capella had to say. He went.

I didn't even feel tempted to stay behind and talk to Capella. Varly had changed my priorities again. I decided that I disliked Caradoc far more than I disliked working for Charlot.

On the way back to the ship, I told Charlot everything. I told him about the battleship, and I told him about the assumption that we had wrong. I expected him to glow with pleasure, but he groaned instead.

"What's the matter?" I asked.

"You were in such a hurry," he said.

"Did I make a mistake?" I asked, my self-satisfaction fading fast.

"*You* didn't," he said, "*but we left them the body!*"

"They can hardly deny that there was a murder," I said.

"That's not the point," he said. "They'll carve that body into thin slices. Whatever there is to be learned from it they'll have before we get a chance. They might beat us to the answers yet."

"Come down right now," I advised him. "It's all getting too complicated. Beat them to the punch. That battleship up there is all the excuse we'll need in public."

He shook his head. "We need your selective agent. We need to know what stopped change on this world. We need evidence of something inimical."

I wondered if the other rounds in the Paradise Game were as difficult to win as this one.

Chapter 10

The maiden's lights picked up the human chain that was blocking the road, and we slammed on the anchors. Johnny had braced himself, of course, but the rest of us lurched forward. Varly hit his head on the windshield, and complained volubly.

Nobody got out. We waited for them to explain. A man came forward and peered into the maiden. It was David Holcomb. He seemed surprised to see so many people crammed into such a small space.

"You'd better back up a hundred yards," said Holcomb, as Johnny wound down both sets of windows. Everything in the maiden was airlocked—it wasn't designed to be a pleasure cruiser.

"Why?" asked Johnny.

"Just back up," repeated the *Aegis* man.

I began to wrestle with the door, and finally contrived to get it open. I stepped out, and let Charlot out. Eve and Nick followed in turn.

"We don't want any trouble," said Holcomb, redirecting his attention to Titus Charlot.

"Why won't you let us pass?" asked Charlot.

Holcomb glanced sideways, as though he were uneasily conscious of Keith Just's presence in the maiden.

"Because in a couple of minutes, it isn't going to be safe to walk around that field. You've got to back up—maybe not more than twenty yards. We don't want anybody getting hurt."

"What have you done?" demanded Charlot.

"You needn't worry about your ship. We checked—it's sealed tight. There's nothing so close to it that it'll be in any danger. It's built to withstand a lot more than the stuff we planted."

"What stuff?" Charlot was livid.

"You forced us to this, Mr. Charlot. We couldn't get a hearing. Nobody was taking a blind bit of notice of us. This is the only way. Now will you please back up, because everything on that field is going to go bang in just thirty seconds."

Holcomb was looking at his watch ostentatiously, to emphasize his point.

"Johnny," said Nick quietly. "Back up fifty yards or so."

"OK, Captain," he said, slipping the maiden into gear and easing her back as he answered. "Aren't you coming?"

Nick took Charlot's arm. "You'd better start walking back, sir. We can argue it out at a safe distance."

Without another word, Charlot turned and began walking back behind the maiden. Fifty yards back, we all stopped. Holcomb and his men had come back with us. Every pair of eyes turned back to face the field. We could see the tall form of the *Hooded Swan* off to one side, and the vast shadows of the Caradoc ships towering over her.

"Get down," said Holcomb. He took his own advice, and dropped face forward onto the grass beside the road. We all followed suit, though Charlot only condescended to crouch in the shadow of the maiden.

I lifted my head so that I could see what was happening.

The lightning beat the thunder by some inestimable fragment of a second. The flash wasn't bright—I blinked, but I wasn't blinded. I felt the shockwave in the ground, but there was only a brief wind in the air— just a hot, dry breath that dried up the few beads of sweat on my forehead.

The initial impression was disappointing. The three big black shadows didn't come tumbling down. It took a lot more than a few capsules of pocket blast to shake a starship. But I knew that bombs had been attached to the

skin of each of those ships, just as bombs had been tied
to every bulldozer and digger on the field. *Aegis* had a
point to make, and they were putting full stops to their
statements in no uncertain terms.

"If you've cracked the shell around one of those piledrivers," I said, "you'll have hot flux all over the field.
It'll leave a scar this world won't obliterate in five
hundred years. Just what the hell are you trying to
prove?"

But Holcomb wasn't taking any notice of me. He was
still looking at Charlot.

"We had to make our presence felt," he was saying.
"We couldn't let you ignore us. We have something important to say and we intend to be heard. People have
got to know what happens here, or our case will be lost
no matter what happens to Caradoc. It has to be *clear,*
you understand? The principles we stand for have to be
planted in people's minds. We couldn't let you hush it all
up. We must make an *example* out of what is happening
here."

"You could have killed a dozen people," Charlot's voice
was flat and emotionless.

"We killed nobody," said Holcomb. "We made certain
there was no one aboard your ship. We searched for
Caradoc personnel. We even tried to make certain there
were no natives in the area surrounding the port. Nobody got hurt."

"There was no *point,*" said Charlot, still unable to
understand. "It's just a petty gesture. It doesn't mean
anything. It's not going to make you any more popular.
It's not going to do a thing for you off this world, and it
certainly won't do anything for you on it. It's senseless."

"It'll show Caradoc we mean business. Not just here
but on every other world where they intend to mount
vast scale operations. We can't stop them, but we can
make them pay. We can cost them, and that means a lot
to them. The one way you can get at a mob like Caradoc
is to destroy its property. Their collective pocket is the
only place where any of them can feel pain. We can put
a bomb in every bit of equipment that Caradoc wants to

use to rape worlds. Anywhere and everywhere. Whether you listen to us or not, whether New Rome listens to us or not, we can still stop them."

Charlot shook his head. "You can start riots," he said. "You can precipitate epidemics of murder. But you can't even make a dent in Caradoc's pocket or Caradoc's plans. Not like this. It just isn't possible."

We went forward to inspect the damage. We fanned out as we went. Johnny nudged the iron maiden into forward motion again, and he trailed us back on to the field. Holcomb was in the vanguard—after all, it was his handiwork that he wanted to survey.

Fires were still burning, and there was a terrible stench of charred plastic and burned machine oil. Where the Caradoc bulldozers had been parked in a neat line there was now a black ridge of debris, with the hulks of the metal corpses sticking out of the mess like camels' humps. Soil had been flung everywhere by the blasts, and everything was filthy. All the paintwork was seared.

The diggers had mostly been left where they were engaged in the job of making holes, and they made individual heaps. Few of them were recognizable—the shovels had all been wrenched free and hurled away, the characteristic lines of their bodies had all been twisted out of shape.

Little apparent damage had been done to the ships—they were all made of sterner stuff. But holes had been blasted in their skins, and the engines in the belly had been pretty thoroughly beaten up. Flux was leaking out of one of the hulls—dripping steadily into a crater, with a slushy tap-tap-tap.

I stood alone in the middle of it all, looking around at the carnage. Nick had rushed to the *Hooded Swan,* but I knew she'd be all right. There'd been nothing within a hundred yards of her, and the *Aegis* people wouldn't have touched her. She could take the blast waves.

Eve came over to stand beside me, and Johnny rolled the maiden to a stop close by one of the Caradoc ships. He got out on the side that was toward me, while Keith Just got out the other side, and held the door while he beckoned to Varly. I was looking at them, and my gaze took in almost incidentally the fact that that particular ship's engines were undamaged.

The possibility dawned almost without reference to consciousness.

"Hey!" I shouted. "Come away from—"

I was interrupted by the explosion. I spun around and dropped reflexively. Eve screamed.

The moment the silence returned, we were all running toward the spot. We shouldn't have been, because where there's one charge which hadn't gone off there might be more, and we ought to have been worrying about our own necks.

Johnny was OK, because the maiden had screened him, and the maiden herself was OK. But Keith Just had been thrown over her front end, and he was laid on the floor like a rag doll. A circle collected around him in no time at all, and a lot of breath was held tight until Charlot slapped the lawman's face and we all heard him moan out a vicious curse.

Within half a minute, he was able to sit up again, and a careful inspection of various bits of his body enabled Charlot to announce that he was only bruised. The charge had been placed right up inside the backblast unit, and most of the shock had traveled downward into the innocent earth.

Holcomb was busy trying to apologize. But his tone suggested that it was only because it was expected of him. I saw Trisha Melly standing near me in the group of anxious onlookers. I caught her eye with mine, and I said: "How do *you* feel?"

She turned her back on me.

Thanks for the fast action, I said to the wind.

—Wasn't necessary, he said modestly.

Thanks anyway, I said. I wanted to press the point because there'd been times in the past when I'd been extremely resentful of his intervention in such situations. Since those times I'd grown to be a little more appreciative of still being alive, and a little less choosy about how my survival came about.

Nick and Holcomb between them got Just to his feet, and everything looked to be distinctly all right.

Until Just collected himself together, looked around expectantly, and said: "Where's Varly?"

Chapter 11

The next morning seemed to be an awful long way away from the one before.

There had been no more murder, despite the provocation offered by Holcomb and his guerrilla tactics. A riot had been averted—but only just. The *Hooded Swan* had been converted into a jail despite the fact that the original bird had flown. Instead of Varly we had the whole *Aegis* contingent in "protective custody." The Caradoc police had rounded them up for Just, but once he had them under his wing he decided to have nothing more to do with Caradoc, and he had deputized Johnny. Personally, I felt that this was not the wisest of moves, bearing in mind that Johnny was an inherently aggressive creature without a great deal of discretion. But there was no doubt that Just could do with some help, and there was no one else available except me. Quite apart from the fact that I had other things to occupy my mind, it wasn't an appointment I would have welcomed.

The problem of what to do about Varly was a particularly thorny one. Capella was all ready to devote his full manpower to a big search, and no one could object to his doing so. But Just felt that he could hardly lend official sanction to such a project. Nor could he mount his own search, having no spare manpower and too much to do anyhow. The only thing he could do was post a "wanted" notice and allow things to take their own course.

To add to the inherent difficulties of the situation yet further, Charlot seemed to be distinctly unwell. We had a conference after breakfast and it was obvious right from the start that he was in no condition to spend the day sifting data out at Caradoc's alien studies section. He sent

Eve and Nick out with instructions to seize as much of Caradoc's records as was humanly possible. We both knew this would be an empty gesture, because if the Caradoc people did know anything, they would most certainly hide it, and we had good reason to believe that they didn't.

As soon as they had gone, he said: "What about this ship that Caradoc has in space?"

I shrugged. "I told you virtually everything last night. It wasn't a very revealing conversation. I inferred—but I could be wrong—that it's a battleship, standing by for orders from Capella. It looks to me as if Caradoc is pre-pared to defend this world against all comers if it can find a good enough excuse. Caradoc's problem is our problem. They badly need something that can stand up in a political brawl. They need a reason for defying the New Rome edict and bringing the ship down. Beyond that, they need some evidence to back up their treaty in court and some excuse for discrediting us. That can always be cooked up, but before they cook it up they want to know exactly what risk they're taking. They want to know exactly how much they stand to gain from this operation. It'll have to be a lot, because it could be very costly for them to begin thumbing their nose at New Rome and New Alexandria both. Personally, I agree with Capella— it's far too big a decision for him. But he's the man with the can to carry home, and he's sweating blood right now. I wouldn't like to guess which way he'll jump."

Charlot looked pensive. "We can't let them have it, We need our play quickly. We have to make it first. I'd lift the *Swan* today and be on New Rome in three days if I thought we had a chance of making a good move. But whatever we tell them, it has to be *right*."

"Why?"

"Because this is only one round. There'll be other worlds, other inquiries. It probably won't be me that has to sort them out, but it will be someone like me, and I have to leave him at least an even chance. We dare not be wrong."

"Look," I said, "you know that the political angles

aren't in my line. I've just never had occasion to walk in the corridors of power where this friendly game of marbles is being played. I don't know where the ultimate authority rests, or how it moves. But it seems to me that if Caradoc wants to start a campaign to rule the galaxy, but is scared in case it gets stamped on, there are much better places to start a fight than here. They're coming from behind —it doesn't affect their position if they wait another year, or another decade. There are always more chances. Surely, the line of least resistance here is for them to back down. Capella's not a moron. He must know that. You must be able to reach him—to talk him into seeing reason. You and he don't need to be on opposite sides. You could sit down *together* and work out your excuses. Nobody in his situation can afford *not* to sell out."

Charlot stared at me somberly. He was leaning way back in his chair, as if his limbs were too weak even to pull him upright.

"Is expediency all you know about?" he asked me.

"No," I said. "I appreciate that there are matters of principle involved. But I can afford to indulge a principle now and again, because the only thing that hangs on my decisions is me. You've got a world dangling at the end of your apron strings. Can you afford principles?"

"Yes," he said.

"After Rhapsody?" I said. "What about the Anacaona? I didn't notice your principles in evidence then. And what about that little matter of paying off my fine, so that you could send me into the Halcyon Drift on a wild-goose chase? Doesn't the word *blackmail* occur to you? Is expediency all *you* know about?"

He closed his eyes. "Do we really have to discuss all this now?" He said. "There are more important things. You know full well that I believe in what I do. The Anacaona are part of something much larger. You may not approve of my experiments but you cannot accuse me of being unprincipled. As to the matter on Rhapsody, I did everything I could to prevent trouble. It was your loyalties that were misplaced. And no one forced you to take a job with me. Your resentment of what I did is understandable, but you cannot object on the grounds of principle. But, please, don't argue with me now. This difference of opinion is immaterial, and we don't have the time. I am not going to try to bribe Capella. I want to see Capella crucified. This drive to run the whole galaxy as a simple commercial enterprise must be stopped. We must have a measure of sanity or there will be war —a war that will kill billions and destroy worlds. Caradoc and its cousins must not be subverted. They must not be tolerated. They must be opposed. If we make that opposition powerful enough, we can save a great deal of killing. I'm not asking you to understand, and I know you won't simply believe me, but you *must* see that we're on the same side, and while you're fighting for me you'll fight *my* way. Is *that* clear?"

I shouldn't have provoked him. I didn't know whether he was right or whether he was wrong. I don't try to decide what's right and what's wrong. I only know what I like and what I don't like. I didn't like Charlot much. I liked Capella less. If I was allied with Charlot, it made sense to commit myself to the same approach. That way we had twice the chance instead of two half-chances.

"OK," I said. "What are we going to do? We haven't time to go through all the garbage Eve and Nick will bring back, and you know it will probably be a waste of time."

There was a pause while his mind changed tracks, and he brought himself back to the problem of finding out what was what in the Pharos life-system.

"We might have got something from a dissection of that body," he said. "But it's too late now, and I don't think I'd make a good job of it anyhow. I think we need a different tack. We can't reason it out, because we don't have the data. But we can make some guesses that might not be too hard to check out."

"Go ahead," I said. "You're the expert."

"We'll assume for the moment," he began, settling himself in his chair, so that I knew we were in for a long session, "that the inferences you drew from the discovery of the fossil carnivore are, in fact, correct. That is to say, this world is a lot older than we thought. We now see the situation in this way: the life-system of the planet evolved for a considerable time in what, for the sake of argument, we shall call the 'normal' fashion. An Earth-type pattern. Humanoid aliens evolved to fill the customary niche. They had reached the stage which we refer to in our own history as 'the stone age.' Right?"

"You don't have to spell it out," I said. "I'm with you all the way."

"I'm spelling it out for my benefit," he said. "I don't want to miss anything by jumping conclusions. We'll take it step by step.

"Now, when we reach the stone age, evolution suddenly comes right away from its 'normal' pathways. Perhaps not so sudden, but sudden enough. Something evolves which rapidly infects the entire life-system from top to bottom."

"Need it evolve?" I asked. "It might have come from outside. Arrhenius spores."

"Where did it come from?" he countered. "It evolved *somewhere*. We've found nothing else like this. It makes far more sense to assume that it evolved here. Now, what is it? We can get a better idea of that by looking closely at what it *does*.

"Quite simply, it pacifies the planet. It reduces all of life here to subjection to a single rule—live in peace. It eliminates all conflict, including sexual reproduction, which is—after all—only a device for promoting conflict and facilitating evolution by natural selection. This new organism—if it is an organism—does away with all that. But it uses two different strategies. Some things become extinct—the large carnivores, the destructive parasites. Others are *modified*—the humanoids, for instance. The animals left alive aren't the ones that just happened to be sapsuckers—they're ones which had the facilities for turning themselves into sapsuckers. And the vegetation had to be modified too, to suit their needs. This is an organized metamorphosis of the entire life-system that we're looking at. Now, what does this suggest to you?"

"Directional mutation," I said.

"That's obvious," he said. "But there's more to it than

that. This new organism may be able to direct mutation, but only within limits. It killed the carnivores, remember. Only *some* of the species were modified.

"But there's a second and more important element to
what this Paradise bug does. It kills, but only in order to
set up a situation where nothing dies. There's a hint of
a paradox here. At what level does this immortality apply? To organisms, certainly, but what about cells? Are
the aliens immortal because their aging cells are continually being replaced by young and healthy ones, or
are they immortal because the cells that they have never
age?"

"If we're going to assume mutational control," I said,
"then the latter seems more likely."

"All right then. If we assume that mutational control
is behind all this, then we have some sort of specification
for our mystery agent. What sort of an organism can control mutations? A virus that unites with the chromosomal
material and gives it the property of self-repair? Perhaps
—but how do we explain these gross changes in the life-
system? How does a virus carry the information necessary to carry out repairs at the molecular level and all
other levels as well, up to and including the whole biosphere? This organism is a sculptor. It's redesigned an
entire ecosystem from the ground up. How can it possibly be so small as to be invisible to the naked eye?"

"Perhaps it isn't."

"Perhaps not." He paused to think. "Suppose we're assuming too much. Suppose it hasn't done all we've
credited it with. Suppose, for a start, that sexual reproduction as we know it never evolved here in the first place.
The male of any species is, when all is said and done, a
spurious luxury. Suppose that on Pharos, parthenogenesis
is and always has been a universal principle. Without
sexual reproduction we can still imagine a moderately
conventional evolutionary pattern—the same kinds of organism evolving to fit the same sorts of niche. The absence
of sexual reproduction would only slow things down—
the absence of recombination would merely mean that

there was a heavier reliance on mutation as a source of variation. And that fits!

"Mutational manipulation could have evolved here as an alternative to sexual reproduction, you see? The material which carries the genetic information and the generative potential on this world—the chromosomes or their equivalent—isn't made up in the same way that it is on most worlds of this type. It behaves *spontaneously* in a different fashion, and it's become stabilized in a different way. It must be self-mutating to a high degree, and instead of coping with mutation by evolving the sexual screening process, it's evolved a different kind of screen, involving some form of testing. All life-systems evolve toward stability—that's what life is: the maintenance of order in an entropic system which tends toward disorder. Our life-system tried one way, the Pharos life-system went a different way. Selective pressure didn't work—or hasn't yet. But mutational control *has* worked—on Pharos, at any rate.

"This world did follow a 'normal' pattern for a long time—it explored the same range of variation. But it explored it in a different way. The Earth-type system is basically dialectic—the present state of variation determines the next, and so on. On Earth, there's no way of scrubbing out the mistakes and trying again. Here, there is. I don't know quite how, but there never has been any real competition on this world. What happened wasn't sudden at all. What I said earlier—that this is an organized metamorphosis—was true in more than a metaphorical sense. This life-system has always been cooperative, like a giant hive. It tried to reach balance through predator-prey situations, but when it failed to reach balance in that way it just went straight back to the drawing boards. It took what it had, got rid of what it couldn't use, and used what it could.

"To build a Paradise."

"You're implying a sort of sentience," I pointed out. "You're saying that this whole life-system is a single unit, and that it knew what it was doing when it metamorphosed."

"I'm ascribing no more sentience to it than to a hive of bees," he said. "I'm implying vast complexity in the generative system, but no more complexity than there is in the Earth biosphere. It's just a different pattern. You're making the old mistake of assuming that if something is ordered there must be logic behind it. Not so. The whole basis of life is that complex patterns form *spontaneously*. Complex molecules grew in the primeval soup just as crystals grow out of their own solutions. Logic is a simulation of the properties of matter, not the other way around. This life-system isn't sentient or intelligent or self-aware —it's totally mechanistic. It doesn't *need* intelligence to create order. It does perfectly well without. It's *our* life-system—the alternative method, or *an* alternative method —which needed intelligence and self-determination in order to become more efficient, and we won't know for a very long time yet that our way works—if it does. In the end, our kind of organism might be forced to discover some kind of direct mutational filter to replace all this messy natural selection. The ultimate destiny of *all* life-systems may not be too dissimilar to this one. We might only be a link in the chain."

"Yes," I said. "Well, before we get carried away into your dreams of how to redesign the universe, can we perhaps consider whether this gets us anywhere right now. If it's true, does it help?"

He had already been carried away, though. This was a theory which fit in well with his own monadist philosophies. For that reason if for no other I was inclined to doubt it. I know caterpillars turn into butterflies, but the idea of an Earth turning into a Paradise didn't strike me as the same sort of thing at all. But I knew that Titus might be right in his inference that we were not dealing with a specific selective agent—a "Paradise bug"—as I'd assumed, but with a property of life itself as it evolved on this world.

The thing was, did it do anything for us?

And the snappy catch answer was: no.

"We have to take this life-system apart," said Charlot. "Take it apart right down to the molecules. From the simple point of view of increasing our own understanding of what life *is,* we must study this system. If we can absorb this knowledge into genetic engineering we could do almost anything."

"Sure," I said, "we can play God. But that kind of thinking runs us right into a blind alley. If this world is that valuable, then it's well worth Caradoc's while to do everything in its power to keep it. You may have cracked the problem, but if you have you've cut your own throat. If I were you I'd start right back at the beginning and find another answer. You mentioned a virus, and then you threw it out. You might well be advised to go back to that virus. With a little bit of fake evidence we can find your universally infective virus for you, and we can quarantine this world. Isn't that exactly what you want?"

"But the virus theory just doesn't stand up!" he protested.

"Perhaps not," I said. "And it's your fight, not mine. If you want to broadcast your theory, you're welcome so far as I'm concerned. But so far as I can see, it doesn't give us much of an angle. Sure, let's by all means make the world special, so that we can claim it for study. But hadn't you better make it worthless as well?"

He was silent, and I could virtually read his tortured thoughts. Sure, Titus Charlot was a topflight diplomat. But he was primarily a citizen of New Alexandria. His principles were those of the Library: the sanctity of knowledge and understanding stands above all things. By all means lie and cheat and steal and blackmail, if it helps in the assembling and understanding of data. But only if it helps. All Titus' rich talk earlier about principles was put in its true perspective now. He had been looking for the truth in the hope—perhaps even with the faith —that it would provide him with a weapon for his cause. Now he had the truth, or what he believed was the truth. But it was pointed at him. What price principles now?

"I'll have to think," he said. "Go away."

"Thanks a lot," I said.

He seemed a bit surprised by the sarcasm. "I'm grateful for your help," he said, as a sort of afterthought. "I really am. It's been extremely useful. It's not that I'm trying to exclude you from the affair now that you've served your purpose—it's just that I need to think in private. I'll tell you what I decide to do."

"Thanks," I said again, and I left. I'm not quite sure why I felt angry about being thrown out just at that moment. Perhaps I was getting delusions of grandeur, and thought that he ought to be hanging on to my every word. Perhaps I was just getting sick of the whole sad affair.

I went to the control room of the *Swan,* mulling over in my mind the account which Charlot had provided as to why this world was the way it was. I had to admit that it looked better than any alternative. I only wished that I knew what might happen next.

In the control room, I set about checking my bug. Obviously, having happened in on the conversation between Capella and his allies in the sky, I hadn't wanted to miss out on future conversations. I couldn't leave the call circuit perpetually open, but I could reroute it into the computer printout system, and I had. All I had to do in order to catch up on the latest news was call it out on the line-printer.

I didn't really expect to find anything—I imagined that Capella wouldn't be in touch again until after dinner. But I was wrong.

There was a brief, formal exchange recorded from ten minutes previously. If I'd left Charlot a bit sooner I could have picked it up live. It was a very different exchange from the one I'd heard the previous night.

Capella had requested the battleship to land, and to deploy its personnel in search of an escaped murderer at large somewhere on the island. The request was very carefully phrased, and mentioned that the peace officer on Pharos had posted a "wanted" notice on the man, but was too busy to organize a search party himself.

I knew full well that Keith Just hadn't given any official backing to Capella's search project, but he hadn't told them not to bother either. Almost any little snippet of conversation between Just and Capella might provide just the ambiguity Capella needed. He was bringing down his battleship in the name of New Rome. Once it was down, Capella and the captain had armed possession of the planet.

I had a nasty suspicion that it would take something on the order of a miracle to make that ship lift meekly into the sky again. Also, knowing what Charlot knew, I had a nasty suspicion that New Rome wouldn't back down meekly by conceding Caradoc carte blanche to rape the planet at their leisure. Step by step, we seemed to be moving closer to an armed confrontation. Perhaps it was just a show of force on Caradoc's behalf. Perhaps they were just testing the resolve of the opposition, without any serious intention of following through. But there was an uncomfortable feeling of inevitability about the attitudes of both sides. If not here, then somewhere else there was going to be a fight.

And the guns would take the place of the excuses.

Chapter 12

I thought the next thing on the agenda just had to be a flaming row between all parties concerned, which would probably end with a cessation of diplomatic relations. But Charlot didn't want that. So far as he could see, the nature of his mission hadn't been changed. He was still looking for a lever to use in the courts of New Rome in the media of every world in the civilized galaxy. It made no difference to him that he was looking for a needle in a haystack that looked ever more likely to catch fire. He knew what he was doing and he intended to do it.

If it was humanly possible.

I stood on the spacefield with Keith Just, and we watched the ship come down. It couldn't land on the tiny area that Caradoc had cleared—with or without bomb craters—and her captain wouldn't want to drop her in the sea or blast a hole a mile in diameter just so he could waste fuel taking off again. He was only making a low sweep so that he could disgorge a percentage of his personnel and equipment into atmosphere. They could make their own way down.

We watched her come in from the eastern horizon, growing bigger and bigger all the while, until she overtook the sun and blotted it out, casting the whole field into black shadow, and surrounding herself with a halo of brightness. She slowed down until she seemed to be inching her way across the sky, and still she grew as she dropped farther and farther.

I could see the awe in Just's face out of the corner of my eye as he misjudged her distance and her size because of her velocity.

Suddenly, while she was still some way from overhead, but still blocking the sunlight with her tail, she shot forth a horde of tiny black dots. She looked like a seed pod bursting, spewing out hundreds of tiny spores. Each one was a copter or a flipjet, and each one was large enough to carry heavy artillery as well as armor and a platoon of men, but as they moved in the shadow of the mother-ship they seemed like a swarm of black flies.

Then the sun was exposed again, and we both had to look away, dazzled. By the time we could see again, the battleship was beginning to shrink as she accelerated and climbed, while the infant fleet grew as it descended, changing appearance momentarily as our prospective adjusted, so that it was first a swarm of bees, then locusts, and then black butterflies.

The mother-ship passed on, and her children became recognizable. We could see the shape of their bodies, sense the whir of rotors, hear the soft buzz of low-power piledrivers. It hardly seemed that they would be able to find space on the field, but as they fell they sorted themselves out into formation, and began to maneuver themselves into a tight bunch. As they sank still farther they began to circle, and then they began to peel off in fours and set down with military exactness in the available space.

The copters came down in rows so tight that there was hardly a yard of clearance between the tips of their blades. They were big—not as big as the *Swan,* but easily of a size with the old *Fire-Eater* and the *Javelin*—the ships I used to fly. Yet these things were fitted in hundreds into the coat-lining of the battleship. I didn't know how many battleships Caradoc possessed, but the mere thought of one would be enough to intimidate most worlds. I knew New Rome had nothing to compare, and I knew that the shipyards on Penaflor had never turned out a monster like that. That ship had been built in space, in the system of Vargo's Star, where the Caradoc operation had its guts, if not its heart. The Engelian hegemony might have half a dozen ships of kindred spirit, and no doubt the other companies were busy putting them together, but I had seen nothing like her before.

As I watched the field fill up with planes, and saw the black dot that was the battleship disappear into the thin tissue of cloud that hung above the western horizon, I realized for the first time exactly what sort of a threat the companies posed. The first power that went out into space had been the power of the Earth governments. If Earth had had only *one* government, like Khor, that power might have proved effective. But as it was, it proved worthless very quickly as colonies seized independence as soon as they became self-sufficient. The power that took over then was the power of know-how—Library power and bureaucracy power. The power to *do* things was completely devalued—everyone had that. The power that mattered was the power of knowing *how* to do them. New Alexandria supplied the worlds, and then New Rome unified them into a civilization. When I had first gone into space, nearly twenty years previously, that had still been a fair picture of the situation. But during those years the companies bloomed like novas. New Alexandria and New Rome had civilized the galaxy—had fed it and nurtured it like a suckling pig—and had created opportunity on a scale hitherto unsuspected. Suddenly, it was possible to own whole worlds. The capacity for growing rich through exploitation suddenly acquired near-infinite proportions. There were no horizons in space. There was a Caradoc Company before I was born, of course—and a Star Cross Combine, and a Sunpower Incorporated—but it was during my lifetime, and my years in space, that their exponential growth gave them such awesome proportions. They had grown to the point where their power was measurable against the power of New Alexandria and New Rome. But it was a different sort of power.

Up to now, the Library and the Law had always contained and controlled the companies. I had always known that there would come a time when the situation would reach a balance—when the companies would try to reverse the containment and the control. I had not expected it so soon.

It wasn't the two years on Lapthorn's Grave that had left me unprepared for such developments—it was a general tendency throughout my life to misjudge the velocity of change. Things happened faster now than they had at any time in history. And we were still accelerating.

I looked out at the serried ranks of Caradoc's pride and joy—at the men in black who were piling out of the copters and the flipjets—and I knew all of a sudden that they weren't playing toy soldiers. This was for real. If it wasn't this world, it would be the next or the next. The glalaxy was full of worlds for the taking, and sooner or later (sooner, it now seemed), Caradoc was going to start just taking them. It had grown too big to be ordered around. Charlot was busy hunting for a miracle to snatch this world from its cavernous maw. He might find one. But not even Titus Charlot could provide ten miracles, or a hundred, to order.

"I guess this is it," said Just quietly. "The war starts here."

"No," I said. "The war started many, many years ago. What starts here is the choice of weapons."

"What the hell am I supposed to do?" he said. "This is illegal. You know it and I know it. So who do I arrest? Capella? The battleship? Just what the hell am I supposed to do?"

"Just be thankful," I said. "Everybody here is sitting on dynamite cushions. You can't do a thing. That's good. If you had an army as well, you'd be carrying the fate of worlds on your bony shoulders. Be glad that you haven't."

"What about you?" he asked, a slight hint of spite creeping into his voice, as if I'd just accused him of being impotent in more ways than one. "What are you going to do?"

"Me?" I said innocently. "It's not my fight. It's not my scene at all. I only work here. My soul is only in hock—it isn't pledged to any side except mine. As for Charlot—he won't fight with fire. The last thing in the world he'd ever think of is leveling a gun at the smallest of Caradoc's minions. He'll fight this on his own ground, and if Caradoc wins he'll simply pack up his ground and move inside. It won't matter to him whether the Library and the Law control the companies or vice versa. He'll try to run the whole show regardless, inside or out, from the top or from the shadow behind the throne."

Just shook his head. "I could almost throw in with those *Aegis* bums," he said. "For all the trouble they've been to me, they're not bad people. At least they have the questions clear in their minds."

"Sure," I said. "They have the questions clear in *their* minds. They have simple minds. Whatever gives you the idea that the questions are *clear?* The questions are as murky as the depths of a stagnant well, and so are the answers. It's just not that easy. It never is. Turn the *Aegis* boys loose—let 'em sink their teeth into this lot. Then we can forget all about them."

"I don't get you," said Just. "I don't get you at all."

"Few do," I consoled him. "Few do."

The Caradoc private army marched away into town. A couple of hours later, they marched back. By that time, Eve and Nick had returned with everything they could steal from Kerman and Merani. They hadn't been able to take the maiden out to the camp, of course, so they'd had to carry most of it by hand. They'd apparently asked for help and it had been provided—in the shape of one solitary Caradoc tech, who must have weighed all of a hundred and twenty pounds. But among the three of them, they had a pretty impressive haul. It would provide Titus with some heavy reading for a good few hours. At least it would mean that he didn't have to leave the *Swan*. Although he wasn't issuing any medical reports, it was fairly clear that he was suffering somewhat. As if he didn't have the odds stacked high enough against him anyway.

When the army came back—not quite so many of them —they got around to sending some people out to us.

The first one to arrive on our doorstep was the security officer, who explained to our anxious ears that he had been ordered to approach Keith Just with a view to cooperating in the matter of dangerous murderers on the loose.

Just, unfortunately, was not in the best of moods, and had taken refuge from the situation in an orgy of self-pity and resentment. The security officer was quite a young man, and although he was probably not innocent of all the evil-mindedness of the Caradoc higher echelons with respect to this affair, he was not an outstandingly nasty man.

Just's only address to him, however, was quite short, and merely consisted of a suggestion that the security officer should do something rather horrible to himself.

The young man did not appear to be terribly offended, nor in the least surprised. As he turned to make his way back to his superiors, probably in order to make preparations for his own search, I called to him to wait.

He half turned, and hesitated.

"If it's any help," I shouted, "he went thataway."

The security officer gave me a dirty look.

I was only trying to be helpful.

About five minutes later, someone else came across to the *Swan*, and was likewise accosted on the doorstep by a small group of people, including myself, intent on stopping him from invading the ship's sacred precincts.

The new arrival was broad, and red-haired, and wore a broad grin that curled at the edges. He didn't have any vast quantities of braid on his uniform, nor any specially ornate insignia, so I assumed that he wasn't important. But he obviously expected his personality to carry enough evidence of his rank.

"I want to see Charlot," he announced. "My name's Ullman."

"You can't," I said. "My name's Grainger."

"I'm the captain of the ship up there," he said, pointing at the sky. "And I'm in charge of this operation on the ground. I have important business to discuss with your boss."

I stared at him for a measured ten seconds, hoping that his grin would falter. It didn't. Finally, I said: "I'll tell the captain you're here."

I called Nick delArco, and left him to look after Ullman. I went to see Charlot myself.

Eve was with him. He'd made a start on the reports—he had them spread out all over the lower deck—and he was giving Eve a careful account of the ideas he'd come up with earlier in the day.

"The battleship skipper's down below," I said. "I've left him with Nick. What's our policy?"

"Ignore them," he said.

"And perhaps they'll go away?"

He looked at me sharply. "I thought that you were too involved with this operation to adopt your customary flippant approach," he said, with deceptive softness.

"Believe me," I said, "if I were to worry about the situation I'd be scared to death. Battleships always bring out my sense of humor."

"Just keep it out of here," he said, but with a hint of resignation in his voice. "Keep these soldiers out of my way, and especially off my back. Let them hunt for the killer and drill on the field to their heart's content. Pretend they don't exist."

"Just's jumpy," I said.

"Forget Just. He's not important. Let Nick take over here—he'll look after things. I want you to go back to Kerman's place. I don't know what we've got here, but it won't give us anything like the full story. Just talk to people, use your eyes and your head. We can't afford not to have a man on the spot, and I'm too busy."

"Do you honestly think it will do any good?" I asked.

"Did you have something else urgent to do?" he countered.

I went back to the alien encampment. Eve went with me—she hadn't got the full story from Charlot yet, but he would have time later for recording his thoughts.

"How ill is he?" Eve asked me, once we were clear of the field.

"So what am I?" I said. "A doctor?"

"You've seen more of him the last couple of days than anyone else," she said.

"We haven't been talking about his symptoms," I told her. "We have a king-size headache here."

"The landing of all those men is bound to count against Caradoc in the courts," she said.

"Sure," I said.

"You don't sound convinced."

"Now there's a thing," I said.

"God," she said. "You haven't changed at all. Not since you were in the port in New York. You've got that same chip on your shoulder and it hasn't shifted an inch. Don't you think for once that you could drop that razor's edge from your conversation?"

"You can't teach an old dog," I said, with a lamentable lack of originality.

"How did Michael manage to stand you for all those years?" she asked.

"With difficulty," I said. And added: "But he hadn't any choice."

"Is that your idea of an excuse?" she asked.

"No," I replied.

We occupied ourselves with such happy and irrelevant exchanges throughout the long walk. The wind never intervened, but I could feel him disapproving all the way. He was another one who believed that I ought to be making gigantic strides in reuniting myself with the human race. He didn't believe that solitude was a reasonable way of life either.

When we got to the camp, I set about making a nuisance of myself in pretty much the way Charlot had intended that I should. I didn't see any reason to be particularly cagey, but on the other hand, I didn't want to tell them anything they hadn't already worked out for themselves. Most especially, I didn't want to tell them anything that might add to their ideas about how valuable the planet was. So I kept quiet about Charlot's theory of a mutational filter replacing natural selection as the principal agent of evolution. My questions weren't quite as guarded as their answers, but I had the distinct impression that we could dance around the point for years without ever getting there.

I stuck mainly with the biologists—the cellular biologists, who might have found some interesting anomalies about the way the beasties were put together at subcellular level. But it wasn't really the level at which my own know-how operated. I was no scientist, just an observer who liked to understand how things worked.

All in all, we got pretty well nowhere except frustrated.

Even so, I kept going, and it was getting close to sunset when we began to head back to the ship.

The forest was very quiet, very peaceful, and very pretty, but I no longer had any trouble with my own personal Paradise syndrome. It no longer looked to me anything like Paradise.

It wasn't, of course, that I'd been put off by what I'd learned about the Pharos life-system. It was just that every twenty minutes or so one of those great big black whirlybirds would do a slow sweep across the nearby tree-tops. They were looking for Varly. And they were having about as much success as we were.

Chapter 13

Instead of going through town, Eve and I elected to take a more direct route through the forest. Its directness was more theoretical than actual owing to the fact that it is impossible to walk a straight line in a forest, and it was undoubtedly slower than the usual route, but time-saving was not our primary objective. We were avoiding people. At least, we thought we were avoiding people.

We had barely gone halfway when one of the copters made a pass over our heads, did a tight turn, and commenced to hover over us while a stentorian voice came over a loudspeaker ordering us to stop or be shot.

We stopped.

The loudspeaker kept on bawling at us, giving out extremely precise instructions as to how still we were supposed to stand, what posture to adopt. It also took time out to tell us exactly what wouldn't happen provided we complied with the suggestions.

It took five minutes for the men in the copter to redirect men on the ground to our position, which gave me, at least, plenty of opportunity to get fed up with standing still waving my fingers in the air.

The search party arrived at the double and surrounded us, pointing their guns at us in a wholly futile display of courage and determination.

The boss was a thin man with a face like a rat and incipient acne. He peered at us both with what I supposed to be a regulation snarl, and decided after due thought and process that neither of us was Varly.

"What the hell you doin' way out here?" he demanded, with an asperity which suggested that we were wholly to blame for the inconvenience caused him.

"It's a free country," I said.

"Don' you know there's a dangerous murderer out here someplace?"

"Son," I said, "I am fully aware of that fact. I have had the doubtful pleasure of having been on this planet for a good deal longer than you. I have had the misfortune of meeting Mr. Varly. I have even had the dubious pleasure of being pushed aside by Mr. Varly. I am not flattered by being mistaken for Mr. Varly. If it is all right with you and your merry men, I would like each and every gun barrel to be redirected to some neutral direction, so that I can continue my walk home. It has been a long day."

"It sure as like hell is not all right with me," he said, mixing his metaphors painfully.

"Well then," I said, "perhaps you'll tell me just exactly what you intend to do about it." I reached out a hand and gently redirected one of the gun barrels with the tip of my forefinger.

"I'm goin' to sen' you home under escort," he said.

"I don't want an escort," I said. "Do you want an escort, ex-Captain Lapthorn?"

"It might be a good idea," she said. "It's getting dark, and we don't want any of these cretins blazing away at us on suspicion."

She had a point. But there were principles at stake.

"I am not going to be shown home by a bunch of feckless kids in black romper suits," I said coldly.

"It's for your own protection," insisted the thin man, who was presumably a corporal or thereabouts, though I didn't know how to identify him from his uniform. "We don' wan' any slipups on this job. We are here to see that nobody else gets hurt here. We wan' to fin' Varly before he kills anyone else an' that includes you. This man is armed and' dangerous."

"There are an awful lot of things aroun' here that are armed an' dangerous," I commented, mimicking his accent in the hope that annoyance would make his acne break out.

"I insist that at leas' two of my men accompany you back to your destination," he said, doubly proud at being able to say "my men" and at being able to pronounce "destination."

I decided that compromise, being the soul of diplomacy, was called for.

"Make it one and it's a deal," I said. "And I'll recommend you for a medal."

He smiled—not because of the medal, but because he thought he'd outmaneuvered me into accepting an escort. One poor unfortunate was quickly appointed to remain with us, while the rest marched noisily away into the forest.

"*Paradise!*" I said. "It'll never recover from this lot."

"We got strict orders not to disturb anything," said the youth with the rifle, looking slightly offended.

"Yeah," I said. "Come on, sunshine, let's go home."

We didn't even get three steps. I heard a thud and turned back to see our intrepid guardian crumpling into a heap. He had been hit on the head by a gun butt.

Varly crouched to retrieve the rifle, and before I could move the hole in the end was pointed at my stomach.

"Hell," I said. "Where did you come from?"

"Keep quiet," he hissed urgently, his expression furious. His close-set eyes were bloodshot and staring. He pointed upward in answer to my question. It could hardly be a coincidence—he must have come in behind the search party. But why? It could hardly be idle curiosity, and he couldn't possible think that there was anyone around that would help him.

"Taking a bit of a risk, weren't you?" I asked. And, in a low whisper, "Who do you think you are—Tarzan?"

"Bastards couldn't catch a cold," he whispered back.

"Possibly so," I murmured. "What now?" Eve, beside me, was very tense. I took hold of her arm and squeezed hard, trying to tell her to stay still. Between us, almost certainly, we could jump him. He knew as well as we did that if he fired the beamer he would have the army down on him in seconds. But I didn't think there was any need for either of us to risk getting hurt.

"Look," he said. "I'll surrender. But keep me away from the boys in black. You can lock me up in that ship of yours, but don't hand me back."

"Well," I said, "I don't know that you need have been so anxious to get to us rather than them. They have a lot to thank you for. If it hadn't been for you, they'd still be looking for an excuse to bring the boys in black down. Just what the hell did you think you were doing?"

"Never mind that," he said, raising the rifle to indicate that he wasn't fooling. "I'm going with you. Turn around and stand apart. Take your hand off her arm, Grainger. Now walk. Stay slow, and stay apart. Anything happens— anything at all—and you'll both get it in the back. I mean it."

A lot of men might not have meant it. But I was ready to believe that Varly did. He was a man habituated to violence, habituated to answering fear with fire. I knew that we were both in dire danger of being burned.

"If they get me," hissed Varly, "they're going to kill me. Just remember that. And they're going to get me if I don't go with you. I got nothing to eat and I daren't try this filthy alien stuff. I got no place to go except your ship. And that's where I'm going."

I didn't bother saying anything lest I should offend him. I often have that effect on people. I kept walking, just like he wanted me to. Eve did the same. Once now and again, I saw her glance sideways at me. That squeeze had given her the wrong idea. She was looking to me to do something—expecting heroics. I'd have thought she knew me better, but could be she had got the wrong idea from misleading accounts of what had happened on Chao Phrya when the spiders had come to tea.

—We can take him, said the wind. The light's dim, his reaction time can't be any too fast. You and I, we have speed. We can take him.

We might beat the beam, I told him, but he's big. I know you can pull some nice gimmicks, but even getting the very best out of me isn't going to put us in the same league with the best of him.

—Come off it, said the wind. We can have him laid out before he blinks. Just let go.

No.

—Coward, he said.

You know better than that, I said.

—It's true.

Maybe. Maybe not. But it's nothing to do with *this*. If I thought it was worth it, I might. But it isn't. Hell—he only wants to turn himself in to someone who isn't liable to string him up. We can afford to do as he says.

—Do you believe that?

Don't you?

—He's not the type. He's hard. There's nothing inside that brain but brutality. He'll force you to the ship, and once he's there he'll keep forcing. He'll push and he'll push until somebody shoots him down. You'd be better to take him here, where there's not the same risk of people getting hurt.

There's two of us, I told him. And he's got a gun in our backs. That's a risk of someone getting hurt. It's a risk I'm not taking. Right?

—Wrong.

It's still the way it's going to be.

He lapsed into silence. Everybody wanted me to be a hero. Well, you don't have to be a hero to stay on the right side of yourself in this day and age, and I was pretty sure that the best thing was to play along. So I kept walking.

We made pretty slow progress, and it took us a lot longer than it might have to get us into the neighborhood of the field. Once we were within shouting distance, we had to be even more careful. Varly knew full well that the field was crawling with black-shirts. But he also knew that the *Swan* wasn't far from the edge.

He made us work our way slowly out around the perimeter, keeping very quiet. By this time it was almost totally dark in the forest, and Varly was breathing down our necks in order to stay certain that he could fry us with a twitch of his finger.

Finally, he stopped us, and then pushed us forward out of the undergrowth. We were hidden from the main part of the field by a low heap of rubble.

"Go forward," he said to me. "Stand straight and walk a dead straight line. I'm going to be right behind you."

"I can't," I said.

I felt the gun barrel drill into my back.

"Why not?" he hissed. His lips were right next to my ear, and I could feel the moisture on his hot breath.

"Because there's a hole there," I told him.

He drew in his breath sharply, and I could tell that he was mad. "Then go around the hole," he said. His voice sounded absolutely tortured, as if he were in pain.

I took one half-stride forward on to the heap of loose dirt, and I felt the point of the gun run right down my spine. I half turned, to glance back. In the darkness, I wasn't sure, and I daren't act on the slender evidence of my eyes, but it seemed to me that Varly was using the rifle for support, with the barrel jammed into the ground. But he knew I'd turned, and he swayed back, bringing the barrel up again.

"Move," he said, his voice rising slightly in pitch and volume, as though it were passing beyond his control.

"Get moving," he hissed. There was faint light glinting off the rifle, and it was glinting off his face as well. He had a high fever. The instant I guessed, he knew that I knew. He dropped the gun from lifeless fingers.

"It's too late," he said. "For God's sake, get me to the ship!" He moved forward, pushing in between us, scrambled his way to the top of the pile of dirt, and fell headlong.

He didn't join the long-dead beast in the hole, but remained atop the heap, sprawled over the ridge in an ungainly spread of arms and legs. His face was upturned, and by the lights that were shining all over the field I could see that it was soaked and twisted. His eyes were open, and red with broken veins in the sclerotic.

"What happened?" said Eve. "What did you do to him?

"I didn't do a thing," I said. "There's something wrong with him."

He was very still. I picked up his wrist very gingerly, and searched for a pulse. I lifted his hand high, and dropped it.

"He's dead," I said.

"Just like that?" she asked, unable to credit it.

"Just like that," I confirmed.

"He looked all right when we first saw him," she said. "That was less than an hour ago. And he sounded..."

"Well, he wasn't all right," I said.

"Whatever he had..." said Eve.

"He's given to us," I finished for her. "Me, at least. Let's get back to the ship."

We left him lying there and we ran back to the *Swan*. The outer lock was open, and Johnny was waiting just inside.

"Get Just," I told him, making my voice sound urgent. "And don't touch either of us."

I pushed Eve into the decontamination chamber, and I got in with her. The jets came on, and we packed all our clothing into plastic bags and sealed them. Then we packed ourselves into plastic bags and sealed *them*. I connected oxygen bottles to Eve's suit and then to mine. I shut the lock from within the chamber, and fried every germ that might be lurking there. Then we came out of the chamber.

Johnny, Keith Just, and Nick delArco were all outside waiting for us. Five was about all the deck could hold.

"I want everybody into the chamber, one by one, in double quick time," I said. "I want everyone into suits. That lock stays shut until further notice. *Nobody* goes out. Nick, you'd better tell Charlot that Varly's outside on the edge of the field and he's died of something not very pleasant. I'm going up to the control room to start broadcasting warnings. I don't know what killed him but I'm taking no risks."

Nick didn't bother hanging around to tell me that Pharos was as safe as they come, that there was no conceivable possibility of infection, that there *weren't* any diseases on Pharos. He knew as well as I did that no risk was worth taking. He went to tell Charlot.

I went up the stairs to the control room as fast as was humanly possible. I sat in the cradle and fixed up a beep that would raise the dead in Capella's place.

I got an immediate answer—they probably had someone on permanent duty keeping in touch with the ship.

He started to swear at me but I stopped him.

"Never mind that," I said. "This is Grainger at the *Hooded Swan*. Find Capella and Ullman as soon as possible, and I mean instantly. Tell them Varly's dead and tell them something killed him. Got that?"

"There's someone on his way," said the voice at the other end. "They'll both know within minutes."

"Right. Then get all this as well. You recording?"

"Yes."

"Varly is on top of a heap of dirt at the edge of the field near the *Hooded Swan*. Don't anyone go near him without suiting up. I don't know what he died of but it killed him in a matter of minutes."

Another voice cut in. "This is Ullman. What the hell is this all about?"

"I'm broadcasting a plague warning," I told him.

"A *plague* warning! You know damn well this planet is clean! What are you trying to pull? You can't get us off this world with a silly damn story like that."

"I don't want you off this world, right now," I told him. "I don't want anybody off this world. It's entirely in the cards that no one will be allowed to leave this world for a long time to come. You'd better get Merani and Kerman and all their boys out here to the field, because there's more urgent work for them to do than playing word games with aliens. They'd better take that corpse apart in a hurry and find out exactly what turned it into a corpse."

"I still think this is a trick," said Ullman.

"Don't be a fool," I said. "What the hell do we stand to gain?"

"It's a biological impossibility for there to be any kind of infection here," he said.

"Well, Varly died of something," I said. "I don't say that it's alien. He might have brought it with him. One of your boys might have brought it in. But one thing's certain—that man's dead, and if I were you I'd get every man on the ground into a decontam suit."

"Well," said Ullman, "That's exactly what we'll do. Every last goddamn man. But you'd better be right."

I switched off the circuit. "Yeah," I murmured. "Or else what?"

Charlot came into the control room, looking grotesque inside his body-shaped plastic bag.

"It's impossible," he said.

"Yeah," I said. "I *know* it's impossible. But I've been in space a good long while, and I know that when you see a man lying dead with an expression on his face like that one had, with the blood and the sweat still oozing out of him, you don't hang around trying to find out how the impossible didn't happen to be impossible after all. You start screaming, and when you've screamed enough, you start praying that you haven't got it. You should be all right—you haven't been outside all day. But I've walked a mile and more with that bastard breathing all over me and it was me had to hold his hand to find out that he was an ex-human. So don't start accusing me of panic. If I'd panicked I'd have spread this thing over every inch of the field by now."

There was a sudden loud beep, and I grabbed at the call circuit switch.

"This is the *Hooded Swan*," I said.

"This is Srinjat Merani," said the other. "I think we'd better keep this circuit open, and hook every man on the ground into it. I've quarantined the camp and asked Ullman to fly decontam equipment out here with all possible speed. We have plague in the camp, Mr. Grainger. The situation is desperate."

You're telling me, I said under my breath.

"Well," I said to Charlot, "it might be impossible, but the miracle which will save Pharos has just arrived in our midst. We have a new problem now."

He looked really sick. I guess I didn't look any too good myself.

Chapter 14

Once everybody aboard was fully clad in transparent plastic, we gathered to discuss the gravity of the situation. By "we" I mean crew—Keith Just and his numerous guests were confined to the lower deck.

By the time Eve arrived, Charlot had already ascertained to his satisfaction that I was not feeling plagued. Despite the fact that I had been all day at the camp and a fair time that evening in Varly's company I did not have a single symptom. So far. This did not, of course, mean that I was in the clear. We knew nothing about the incubation period of whatever it was that had killed Varly.

"How are you feeling?" Charlot demanded of Eve.

"All right," she answered, sounding a little apprehensive.

"You mean that?" he persisted. "This is no time for valiant courage. Do you feel anything?"

"There's nothing wrong that I can detect," she said.

"Captain?"

"I'm fine," said Nick. "A little tired, but apart from that I've never been fitter."

"Johnny?"

"Not so good," said Johnny. There was a sudden profound silence. This was the answer that no one had expected. Eve and I had been exposed, Nick could well have encountered the bug any time during the last couple of days. But Johnny hadn't been off the field since the first day except when he had accompanied the rest of us into town. If anyone should have escaped, it ought to be Johnny.

"How do you feel?" demanded Charlot, his voice cold and cutting.

"I've been bad for three or four hours," said Johnny. "Nothing much—didn't seem to be serious. Just an upset stomach, mild diarrhea. I feel a bit hot, and my mouth's dry, but that might be the worry."

"It can't be the same thing," I said. "It killed Varly in a matter of an hour."

"Don't be a fool," said Charlot. "How do you know how he was feeling when he first picked you up?"

"True," I conceded unhappily. My comment had been motivated by hope and the desire to reassure Johnny rather than by medical confidence.

"Now think'" said Charlot. "During the last two days, have you done anything at all that might have exposed you—and only you—to any kind of disease-carrying agent?"

It was a difficult question. What, on Pharos, could possibly be a disease-carrying agent? Nothing to bite him, nothing to sting him. The only disease-carrying agents on Pharos, so far as we knew, were ourselves. And it was a dead certainty that nobody from Caradoc or *Aegis* would be carrying anything like what had killed Varly.

"There was the fight," said Johnny. "I picked up some bruises. I guess that's the most likely. I messed about in some of the Caradoc diggings, but I showed Grainger what I found there, and some of the Caradoc men were down in the hole at one point, looking at the bones. The only other thing...but that couldn't have been it."

"Tell me," demanded Charlot. "I'll make the judgments."

"This morning. I was...talking, you know, just...playing about...with some of the aliens. They came out of the forest to look around. I just wanted a close look at them."

"No good," I said. "We've all been hobnobbing with aliens longer than that."

"Varly's last-known contact was an alien," said Nick. "He killed one."

"Merani and his team have been working closely with the aliens," said Eve, sounding just a fraction stricken.

"They've been working with them for months," I said.

"I've been in contact with them. So has Titus. And the *Aegis* people."

"Just a minute," said Johnny.

Silence fell again. We all thought he'd remembered something else—we were all waiting for the vital revelation.

"The *Aegis* people," he said. "Some of them . . . I think they had diarrhea too."

"But they've been locked up down there!" I protested.

"That's right," said Johnny. "The only people they could have caught it from today are me and Just. But yesterday...they were anywhere and everywhere."

"Stay here!" ordered Titus. He strode out of the control room and clattered down to the lower decks.

"At this rate," said Nick, "we could all have it."

"Thank *you*," I said. "Line up on the left to drop dead. Do you want to run a sweepstakes on who's still alive at daybreak?"

"Shut *up*," said Eve.

The conversation died.

Charlot returned a couple of minutes later. "We're in bad trouble," he said.

"We know," I said.

"How many?" asked Johnny.

"Four," said Charlot. "Just sickening. Nothing serious, they thought. They feel bad, but not very. Four of them. And Just."

Eve buried her head in her hands. During all the time that Varly's gun had been pointed at her back she hadn't looked one tenth as scared as she did now.

"It doesn't make sense," I said. Somebody had to say it. It was a pretty hollow thing to say, while we were all sitting there contemplating disaster and doom, but damn it, it *didn't* make sense—not at all. There was no logic to it. Four *Aegis* people, plus Just, plus Johnny, plus God only knew how many at Merani's encampment all felt ill. Not seriously ill—just ill. The sort of thing you could pick up on almost any world, and almost invariably did. Changes of air, changes of water. Hell, you could pick up a fragile gut by traveling ninety miles across country. I'd had symptoms such as Johnny was describing on a hundred occasions.

But no one had suffered on Pharos before now. The Caradoc people had been here months, the *Aegis* people weeks, our own group only days. All of a sudden, this bug had found us out. And something—could it really be the same bug? —had killed Varly. Justice, maybe, but enough to throw a flat panic into every single man (and woman) on the planet.

What had happened today? Only one thing. The battleship had dropped a thousand men. Enough to introduce fifty million minor bugs to the planet's surface. But the disease had broken out in exactly those places where the Caradoc black-shirts *hadn't* gone—the alien camp, the *Hooded Swan*. And Varly. The invaders had certainly never got near *him*.

What had happened yesterday? What did Varly, the *Aegis* people, Johnny, Just, and the scientists at the waterfall have in common on that day? Nothing. Absolutely nothing.

It didn't make sense, and I said so.

"Captain," said Charlot, choosing to ignore me, at least for the time being. "I want a section of the lower deck sterilized, and then prepared as an isolation section, with a lock that can be decontaminated every time someone goes through it. I want everyone with any symptoms at all in that section, but keep the suits on for the time being, just in case they don't all have the same thing. Just takes charge inside the section, you take charge outside. We'll get a doctor from Ullman—or transfer our cases to their isolation sector if they haven't a doctor to spare just for us. Miss Lapthorn will help you. Grainger, you come with me. We're going out to find what Caradoc is doing about that body."

"What about the call circuit?" I asked.

"Check with the rest now. Then one of the *Aegis* people who isn't ill can take over and maintain a permanent contact."

"*Aegis* people! In the control room?"

"It's only a temporary measure," said Charlot. "I'll be back here shortly even if you have other things to do."

That reminded me.

"How do *you* feel?" I asked him.

"Bad," he said. "Probably worse than the ones who are properly sick. But I haven't got what they've got."

"Are you sure about that?" I said. "You're the only case of illness on this world we know about prior to today."

"I assure you I haven't been spreading any plagues," said Charlot, in a voice that was as dry as charred paper. "I have not been ill—merely somewhat decrepit. Yes, I know what you're thinking—there's no need to annoy mc further by suggesting it. Of course I could be wrong. Of course I could be dead within the hour. But you'd better hope fervently that I'm right, because if I'm not, who is going to get us all out of this mess? Kerman? A military doctor from the battleship who never saw Pharos until today? You'd better pray that I stay healthy, Grainger. Now check that circuit and let's move."

Wordlessly, I turned to activate a bleep at all points on the circuit.

"Merani here," came one instant acknowledgment.

"This is Powell. I'm in town," said the second.

"*Harrier 32*," said someone else, presumably giving the name of a craft rather than a person. "Just a second. Ullman wants to talk to you."

"Never mind the second," I said. "This is the *Hooded Swan*. We have six cases of reported illness here. None apparently serious."

"We have nearly thirty cases here," said Merani. "Some are only slight. At least ten are serious—two may be critical. No deaths yet."

"Ask him how long since the outbreak started," said Charlot.

I relayed the question.

"Nobody reports feeling ill prior to this morning," said Merani. "The first cases—cases which are now critical— were in the biology section. They reported sick in the early evening, before you left the camp. It was some hours before the seriousness of the situation was realized."

Fools, I muttered under my breath. "Who's in charge there?" I asked, letting the sting loose into my voice.

"Kerman," he replied.

"Kerman's not ill?" I asked.

"No. Perfectly fit. Is this really...?"

"No," I said. "Powell—you got a report?"

"No figures," he said. "The military has taken over here in town. Ullman has gone back to the field...."

"This is Ullman," said a new voice, cutting across Powell. "I'm taking charge of the whole operation, Mr Grainger. This whole planet is now under martial law. You people are instructed to stay inside your ship. I have a full medical team working on the problem, with the cooperation of the medical team from the town. We'll have the problem licked in no time."

"You can go to hell," I said. "Who the hell do you think you are? *Martial law*!"

"Stay in your ship," repeated Ullman.

Charlot put his hand on my shoulder and leaned forward.

"I warn you, Ullman," he said. "If you interfere in any way with me, people on this world are going to die. A great many people. This isn't a medical problem—this is a problem in ecosystemic analysis."

"Rubbish," said Ullman. "No one in my crew or in the town has reported anything more serious than they could have given themselves with a dose of laxative. Hell, I've been on a hundred worlds, and I usually feel like this first day down. I'm not incapacitated in any way. If this is a plague, then I'll be among the first to die, and you can take over then. In the meantime, I'll run things. Got that?"

"Ullman," said Charlot steadily. "If you have contracted this disease you are in deadly danger. You are in no position to throw your weight about. You are quite correct in saying that you might well be among the first to die. Varly is already dead."

"He didn't die of gut ache," said Ullman.

"Do you know what he did die of?"

"I've got surgeons and bacteriologists taking him apart right now," he said.

"I'll be there in two minutes."

"If you try I'll have you forcibly restrained."

"You might just as well cut your own throat. Don't try to make a hero out of yourelf, Captain Ullman. The smallest measure of common sense should tell you that you can't possibly win your little game now. You're beaten on this world. I haven't beaten you—the world has. I'm on your side, now, Captain. Somebody has to save your life. All your lives. You can't do it. I don't know how much *real* faith you place in your medical teams, but believe me, they can't handle it. Ask them, Captain. You're in trouble."

"You're trying to make a fool out of me," said Ullman. "I don't know what killed that man, but I know with absolute certainty that it isn't what I've got. I've had this before, I tell you. You know as well as I do this is *normal*. You're taking advantage of a sensitive stomach to try to throw the fear of death into all of us. It won't work, Charlot."

"Captain Ullman, answer me one question. How many men in the town are exhibiting exactly the same symptoms as your crew? They've been here months. You know that."

"And *you* know full well that the moment anyone broadcasts a plague warning every lazy sod with a pimple starts believing he has typhoid fever. *You* started this plague, Charlot. You and your crazy plague warning. There's not one of my men who has anything in the way of *real* illness to report. I know what they've got because I've got it too, and it's nothing, and you're not going to scare us with it. We'll all be all right by morning, and until then my medical teams will keep everything under control and you'll stay in your bloody ship."

"What about the men at the camp, Ullman? And tell me this—how many of your men, and Capella's men, have this imaginary sickness?"

"That's irrelevant," said Ullman.

"Like *hell* it is," intervened a third voice, loudly and apparently on the verge of hysteria. Merani.

"How *many*?" demanded Charlot.

"I'll tell you," said Powell. "There's a doctor here with me now. We have two hundred and fifty men here, Ullman has nearly a thousand. That makes more than twelve hundred men. Seven hundred have reported sick. *Seven hundred.*"

"All with bellyaches!" howled Ullman.

"I'm coming out," said Charlot. "I'm bringing Grainger with me. We're going to talk to your doctors, and we're going to find out what that postmortem's turned up. Don't try to stop us, Captain Ullman."

He didn't switch off the circuit. He just stood back from the console and turned away toward the door. I followed him. We left the strains of angry conversation drifting out into the now-empty control room. Ullman wasn't popular—not popular at all. For what it was worth, Caradoc seemed definitely to have lost this round of the Paradise Game. Merani and Powell—whoever he was—were all ready to throw in the towel. So were seven hundred others. Ullman hadn't a chance. But we had a new game to play now. The Paradise Game had turned into Beat the Devil.

Chapter 15

We found the copter to which they'd taken Varly's body without too much difficulty. No one gave us any directions, but nobody tried to stop us either.

Ullman wasn't there. I concluded that either he thought discretion was all-of-a-sudden the better part of valor, or his attack of the runs had suddenly taken a turn for the worse. Personally, I didn't care much either way.

Varly was nothing but a gory mess by now. I couldn't stand to look at him. They'd taken him apart with ruthless efficiency and great effect. I was glad that I was sucking an oxy-bottle inside a plastic bag—I had an idea that I might not be able to stand the smell.

Everyone else was in plastic bags as well. There were about a dozen of them, and they were all going like the clappers. Not that anyone was doing anything particularly hurried, but they all had a look of intensity about them, and an ice-cold efficiency about their motions, that suggested they were stretching themselves to their utmost.

The copter was full of equipment like surgical waldoes and microanalytical equipment, and most of it was, or had been, in use. I had to admire the way that Caradoc had kitted the thing out, even bearing in mind that its primary purpose was probably to put soldiers back together after they had been blown apart, so that they could go and be blown apart again.

The only man who had enough attention to spare to even notice that we'd come in was the coordinator. He recognized Charlot instantly, though he'd never seen him before in his life. He shook hands warmly and told us how much he appreciated our help. I thought he laid it on too thick, but he was a refreshing change from Ullman. Either

119

he had a different approach to life or he'd learned enough from the corpse to know that his bread was well and truly buttered on the black side. He introduced himself as Markoff.

"What killed him?" demanded Charlot, cutting off the flow of irrelevancy with a gesture.

Markoff suddenly became very serious indeed.

"I'm sorry," he said. "I'm overreacting. I think. But this is enough to...I'm afraid the question isn't 'What killed him?' at all. It's more like 'What didn't?' "

I could tell that Charlot had no patience whatsoever with the doctor's wordiness. I knew the type—big, bluff, bearded, life and soul of any party, the kind of man who loved to help and be appreciated. I could tell from the way he rabbited on now that this was as bad as it could be. But Charlot, if he understood, didn't give a damn about the big doctor's personality problems.

"*What killed him*?" he repeated, his voice like a whiplash.

"So far," Markoff said unhappily, "we've found three different viruses. And three different bacteria that carry them."

"The viruses are of Terrestrial origin?"

"I'd say definitely, but for one thing. All three are DNA viruses—fairly large, as viruses go, with complex protein coats. But we can't identify any of them. Not one of them is known."

"But they are DNA viruses?"

"Yes."

"So they couldn't possibly have originated here, on Pharos?"

Markoff made as if to shrug his shoulders, but thought better of it. "You know more about the life-system here than I do," he said. "This viruses definitely contain DNA, which so far as I am aware is absolutely characteristic of the Earth biosystem. But I've seen nothing like these bugs before."

"Nothing like them?" queried Charlot.

"Well," said Markoff, "insofar as one virus is pretty

much like another, they're not dissimilar to known types. But they aren't those known types."

"What about the bacteria?"

"The same story," he said. "Two cocci, each about two microns in diameter. One bacillus, six microns long. Chemically, almost certainly of Terrestrial origin. All unknown."

"But similar to known types."

"Very. But none of the known types that they're closest to is pathogenic. And none is known to act as a carrier for a virus. Hell, these viruses aren't phages—they're just hitching a ride in the bacterial cells. These are human-infective viruses, Charlot—unknown human-infective viruses carried by unknown bacteria. Now does that make sense to you?"

"Yes," said Charlot.

"Well, I wish you'd explain it to me."

"They're mutant."

"That's impossible. Are you seriously expecting me to believe that in a matter of days, six new species, not only co-adapted but adapted to a whole new mode of life, have arisen by pure chance mutation?"

"Chance," said Charlot, "had very little to do with it."

"You're talking in riddles."

"This world has a unique life-system. It doesn't evolve by natural selection. It evolves by mutational filtration. Terrestrial microorganisms—perfectly harmless, free-living Terrestrial microorganisms—imported into this world by the Caradoc vanguard have been adopted by the indigenous life-system and converted into lethal pathogens. I don't know how and I don't know why, but that's what's happened. The important thing is—what can we do about it?"

"We can prepare specifics to knock out these bacteria. That's easy enough."

"The bacteria aren't the problem. What can we do about the viruses?"

"We can immunize. But it's a bit late for that. We'd need a specific immuno-serum for each virus, which will take time to prepare, and when it's prepared it will only protect men who aren't infected against infection by that particular bug. If this life-system is mass-producing these bugs, we haven't a hope of preventing all infection. And even if we had, we could only protect a tiny minority of the personnel on surface. More than half of them are already infected, if the information circulating via the grapevine is correct. Once the virus is *in situ* there's nothing we can do about it. We can only prevent virus infections—we can't cure them. We can treat the symptoms as they appear, but heaven only knows whether that'll do any good. These bugs took that man apart in the space of two virus generations. Half a dozen cells were initially infected, they produced several million viruses each and lysed—the secondary infection was almost total. His blood turned to garbage just like *that*."

Markoff snapped his fingers loudly. It was a horrible sound. It wasn't a very nice thought.

"There's one small thing," I said. "If these things are so incredibly potent, why did nobody catch them till today, and why do most of the victims appear to have nothing worse than an upset gut?"

"The first's easy," said Markoff. "If these bugs have been deliberately turned out to definite specifications, they weren't just turned out in a spare moment. I don't know how any kind of a mutational filter is made to work, but one thing I am certain of—to turn a harmless bacterium into a deadly killer to order takes thousands of generations, whether it's the struggle for existence that evolves them or some weird intracellular gimmick. As for the second, though..."

"These bacteria," said Charlot. "Two cocci, one bacillus. They're not all mutations of a single original, then?"

"It's only an opinion," said the bearded man, "but I'd say no. The viruses as well. They don't have a common ancestor. They're modifications of different models, I'd say."

I saw what Charlot was getting at.

"The timing," I said. "All the men with bellyache have got the mark one. Varly picked up the marks two, three, and four."

Charlot shook his head slowly. "No," he said. "There's too much method in this for a sloppy explanation like that.

Far too much. This was a simultaneous release of several different types of organisms. Organisms carefully tailored to just one purpose. . . . No! More than one purpose. They're big viruses, you said. Complex. Carrying more genetic information than would be required for a simple, single-minded killer. We mustn't assume the hand of chance in this at all. This life-system has an absolute stranglehold on chance. There's absolutely nothing haphazard about the way Pharos went about putting this thing together. Varly's not the only one infected with the killers. Every man who's sick is carrying the same little bundles of instant death, but they're lying dormant. Not only that—every man who *isn't* sick is carrying them too, but not even dormant. There are three stages of virus infection—the particle itself, the virion; the genetic element in attachment to the chromosomal material; and the full-scale subversion of cellular activity.

"The reason why ninety-five percent of those affected are showing nothing more than minor gut sensitivity is because they haven't *got* anything worse than a harmless gut infection. The disease that killed Varly is only incipient. We—you and I and the rest of the healthy ones—haven't even got that. In us, the bacteria and the viruses are completely quiescent. No virus infection, no bacterial multiplication preparatory to virus infection."

"It still only half makes sense," I said. "That may well be a very accurate account as to how things are happening, from a medical point of view. But it lacks logic."

Charlot looked into my face, and behind his watery eyes I could practically see the relays clicking at the speed of light. But there was a hint of rage and disappointment about his expression which told me that it didn't compute. He was riding high as a kite on the tide of his own genius, but he couldn't quite solve the equations. He knew what was happening, and I was as sure as he was that he had it all figured right, but the answer just wouldn't fall out. Always and forever this world was just one step ahead of Charlot's logic. We kept finding more and more, digging deeper and deeper, but it just wouldn't fall out.

"It's here," he said, cupping his hand. "But I just can't quite grasp it."

The tone of his voice suggested that he believed his illness to be responsible for the fact that he couldn't quite grasp it. It was obvious that he thought he *ought* to have the whole thing off pat. He might have been right. A healthy Charlot might have anticipated this two days ago and stopped the whole thing. Who could tell?

"Let's not, for the moment, bother about why," I said. "Let's think whether there's anything constructive we can do about it."

"I agree entirely," said Markoff, who had been visibly put out by Charlot's pent-up emotion and gesture of frustration.

"Prepare the immuno-serums," said Charlot.

Markoff nodded. "That is already being done," he said. "A matter of course. But so many of them ... a thousand men and more to treat ... we have only limited facilities here. It will take time we simply do not have. We will also treat the symptoms of those who are ill as they appear. But this too takes time, and men, and facilities which we do not have. There is a limit to what we can accomplish. There will be no miracles."

Charlot nodded agreement. "There will be no miracles."

A soldier appeared from the airlock, with an expression of some agitation on his face.

"Dr. Markoff!" he said.

"Get out," said Markoff, hardly glancing toward the man. "I told you that I was not concerned with Captain Ullman's demands and I am not."

"It's not that," said the soldier. "Ullman's collapsed. A few moments after he finished speaking over the call circuit. He's unconscious. We moved him to his bed, but I think he's dying."

I exchanged a glance of surprise with Charlot. This was the man who had held out to the last against believing in the plague. I could hardly have thought of a more appropriate second victim, if there had to be a second victim. But why Ullman? What had triggered the virus from stage one to stage two?

"Oh, my God," I said suddenly. "I know why."

"Why what?" asked Markoff.

"I know why the diseases behave the way they do."

I paused, not because I wanted to create suspense, but because I wanted to sort out the words.

"Look," I said. "Varly is dead. He killed an alien. The plague struck hard out at the scientific camp—among the biologists, not the linguists. Four *Aegis* people are sick. Four *Aegis* people were involved in blowing up the Caradoc equipment. Johnny is ill. Johnny was in a fight with one of the Caradoc men. Over half the soldiers are ill—professional soldiers. Ullman collapsed—moments after throwing a fit of anger at us. We didn't get the law of life quite right, Titus. It's: *Live in peace or not at all.*"

"The complexity of the virus," murmured Charlot, thinking it over. "A trigger which responds to aggression. Specific physiological changes associated with anger, with killing, with destructive impulses. Why the biologists?"

"They killed specimens," I said. "For dissection, for analysis. Everyone else was specifically forbidden to kill. This life-system is so perfectly ordered. It canceled death. We brought death back. It's canceling us. Every act of aggression, of violence, of anger...

"Jesus," I finished. *"Just think what would happen if we took these viruses back to the stars!"*

Chapter 16

Johnny didn't look too bad. It was, after all, no worse than a case of seasickness. So far.

I told him what we thought. It took some time, because he didn't really understand about the viruses and the bacteria. But I did manage to get across to him that he had better keep his temper in check and think only pure thoughts from here until further notice—perhaps forever.

"Will we ever be able to leave?" he asked.

"I don't know," I said. "The battleship's sent for help from New Alexandria, but it'll be a week or more before anyone gets here. And then it'll be a matter for someone else to decide whether anyone is allowed to land or not. In the meantime, all the Caradoc people are doing everything they can."

"How many dead so far?"

"Only four. Varly, Ullman, two biologists. Some others have had a worsening of your sort of symptoms, but either the bugs were just flexing their muscles or it was a friendly warning to those concerned to repent of their sins or else."

"I guess everybody is pretty scared of their own feelings," said Johnny.

"You said it, boy. Hell, when I think back to picking those flowers without a qualm and casually dropping them on the ground as if it didn't matter a damn. And that shouting match I had with Holcomb. . . .

"I guess I must be a nice guy deep down after all. Maybe Pharos approved of my motives. After all, though this isn't quite the time for even my sense of humor, it's the thought that counts, you know."

He didn't laugh. It had come to that. Nobody dared

laugh. Nobody who believed us, that is. We'd tried to distribute the good news, or the terrible news, depending on what sort of temperament you might have, to the best of our ability, but we hadn't met with a very good reception. The army just wouldn't credit it, despite the evidence of Ullman's corpse and the testimony of their own medical officer.

There was no doubt, however, that I was right. If I'd needed any further evidence to support me it was right under my nose. I'd watched Charlot seethe with fury because he couldn't supply the answer that was within his reach all the time. Now he was down with stage one—gut ache and the runs, and he was pulling out every last inch of his masterful self-control. In him, though, it was a fraction more serious. He had been one degree under to start with, and he could well have done without this extra burden.

We had extended the sterile section on the bottom deck of the *Swan* quite considerably, so that the sufferers could each have privacy if they needed it. The last thing we wanted was for them to get on each other's nerves. On the other hand, we also didn't want them getting neurotic in isolation. It was a tough problem, but all we could do was make the information and the assistance available, and let people use it as they would.

Never in my life before had I spent such a considerable length of time making such a considerable effort to be nice to everybody, and never in my life before could I have succeeded so well.

Johnny, especially, seemed to welcome my company once now and again. I'd always been aware of the fact that he thought somewhat more highly of me than logic would have led him to, but the incidence of the Pharos plague completely changed my attitude to that tinge of hero-worship.

I had never actually *liked* Johnny previously. All of a sudden, I did. It was not simply a matter of pretense for the benefit of his health. I actually did like him. It is remarkable how changeable one's character actually is, when circumstances encourage change.

"How are the anti-sera coming along?" he asked. Two days had passed since that long, sleepless night when the plague first struck. A sort of deathly hush had lain over all human activity in the meantime. I'd heard of people scared of their own shadows, but this situation was something far more deep-seated than that.

"Slowly," I told him.

"How many do we need now?"

"Five. Markoff is pretty sure that we've tagged them all now. It's probable that there would have been a great deal more if the plague warning hadn't gone out so early."

"How very modest of you to say so," said Johnny.

"No credit due to me," I said. "If it's due to anyone, it's due to Varly. He was the one obliging enough to commit murder and thus alert us to the seriousness of the situation within a matter of hours."

"How did the thing spread so fast in one day?" he asked. "I can't see any infection pattern. Who spread it?"

"Nobody spread it," I said. "The Pharos life-system worked like one great big unit—which, of course, it is—and gave us all one great big infectious blast. There was no infection pattern, except possibly here on the field, where the nearest Pharos organism was some distance away. But there were the aliens, remember—the innocent, harmless, lovely aliens that you talked to that day. And many others, I don't doubt."

He nodded. "I see," he said, and then, after a brief pause, "I swear I'll never start another fight, no matter what anyone says to me."

"Yeah," I said, not allowing the least trace of sarcasm or cynicism into the intonation. "When this is all over, if it ever is, remind me to tell you I told you so. It could have been worse, you know. If you'd had that fight two days ago instead of four, you could be dead."

"I don't see how it picked me up after the event anyway," he said. "Or was it just taking exception to my general character?"

"Appearances can be deceptive," I said. "I don't really feel that this thing is a great judge of morality, though.

The trigger is definitely chemical—I think you were still harboring resentment over the fight—mulling it over in your mind—reliving it partially in your memory. That's what caused the physiological reaction which started phase one. Just think about pleasant things from now on, hey?"

"I'll bet you, you can't *not* think of a white horse for five minutes," he said.

He was, of course, in a hell of a situation. When you know what not to think about, how can you avoid having it perennially on your mind? But attitudes are all important. When Johnny thought about that fight now, he wasn't thinking "I should have done *this* to the bastard, and *this*, and if he ever . . ." Not at all. He was now thinking along the lines of "Why ever did I let the guy get me all steamed up?"

Personally, I thought we should have filled every man who was sick up to the brim with happy. juice and kept them under heavy sedation while the rest of us fought the problem. I reckoned there were enough spare men who were useless so far as the medical efforts went—me included—to look after a few hundred sleepers. But Charlot and Markoff between them had decided not to release their stocks of the sedative drugs, except in cases where a real need could be seen. I could see the reasoning behind it—supplies were finite, if apparently abundant, and we *might* be here forever—in which case our rations of those drugs might take on an entirely new significance. They were thinking in the long-term, despite their air of guarded optimism any time anyone approached them and asked for a progress report. I thought that was significant.

"You know," said Johnny, "I think we all must be a little bit crazy. The worse that can happen to us—the absolute worse, is that we're condemned to life in Paradise, and guaranteed a peaceful time and a life of pleasant harmony. That's it. Sometimes I wonder why we're fighting quite so hard and with such determination."

And of course, he was right. This was the dream,

wasn't it? This was the dream that was behind the Paradise syndrome, which motivated the Paradise Game, which was the whole thing behind the initial trouble on this world. So what was so hateful about it?

But like I've said before, I don't believe in Paradise. I don't like the Paradise Game. I think the whole thing is a farce and an illusion.

If I'd wanted to exult about being proven right, Pharos was offering me every excuse. But in situations like ours, you get to be just a little bit afraid of exultancy. You get to be just a little bit afraid of everything you are. The fact that the virus hadn't even begun counting strikes against me on the road to hell didn't mean that I was a prime candidate for Heaven. The guy who got his lily-white mitts on the Holy Grail in the old legends might have loved it here. But for us poor humans . . .

No chance.

"That's right," I said to Johnny, in a voice that was only slightly sad, and a little bitter in spite of myself. "It's the nicest place in the galaxy to be condemned to. One hell of a lot better than the *last* place I thought I was going to spend my whole life."

That last place, of course, was Lapthorn's Grave, the hunk of bleak rock on the edge of the Halcyon Drift. That place had done bad things to me, but I wasn't altogether convinced that Pharos wasn't doing worse.

As I left Johnny, ready to go back to my assigned work in plague-fighting, I met Trisha Melly. She still didn't want to seduce me, but at least she didn't mind talking to me, which was more than I could say for Holcomb.

We exchanged a few words. She was a real little ray of sunshine. A dyed-in-the-wool idealist. She had found a real bright side to look at. She thought that as a matter of duty we ought to lift our ships and take our glorious gift back to the whole of galactic civilization. Live in peace, or not at all. She thought it was our destiny.

She might have been right.

In my most amusing moments, I thought it might be our just deserts. But I knew the human race would never stand for it. It would fight the plague with everything it possessed, and it would win in the end. I was dead certain that we weren't booked for a universal Heaven just yet.

Chapter 17

In the two days that followed there were no more deaths, but the steady trickle of men reporting the initial symptoms continued. By dawn on the fifth day after the plague warning there were less than a hundred men and women remaining apparently healthy. No one had recovered, or made the slightest step toward recovery. A good many cases seemed to get worse, but it proved to be a simple worsening of the symptoms already extant, and no one could say that it was the bugs rather than the worry. I half expected that sooner or later some fool would precipitate himself into the final phase of the disease simply by virtue of fear that he might, and start a panic which in turn killed more people. But that didn't happen. The Pharos viruses were inordinately sensitive—they were not activated by fear, or any other strong emotion except anger and the urge to destroy. Those of us who were able to work—including a good number of those who were supposedly ill—did so, in search of some miracle agent that would clear all our systems of all the killer bugs. It was like searching for the panacea, or the philosopher's stone.

But we had extra help.

It was help that no one knew about except me, and I had no intention of telling anyone else. If the wind managed to turn the trick, I intended to take all the credit for myself.

I had, in the past, been inclined to neglect the wind. In the beginning, I had ignored him as much as was possible, in the fond but forlorn hope that he might go away. As I had become reconciled to his existence and his persistence, I had moved from rejecting him to taking him for granted. So far as I was concerned, he was just an inner voice—an invisible companion. I tended to treat him, and think of him, as if he were human—which was true, in a way. Humanity had been thrust upon him. He was manifest as a humanly-organized mind. I had always been aware that he had talents above and beyond my own, but I had always felt uncomfortable in their presence, and I had not inquired deeply into their precise nature. Nor had I concerned myself with determining his exact existential status, the secrets of his life-cycle and personal organization. I did not even know what he was made of.

Perhaps it is odd that I had never evolved any curiosity as to these things, as I have a naturally curious outlook. But I have never had a personality that absorbed things into itself. Lapthorn used to be like that—everything he touched made an impression on his soul. He not only wanted to understand things, but also to feel them, to identify with them. My understanding was of a different kind—cold, aloof, mechanical. I am basically a pragmatic man—I am neither emotionally self-indulgent nor spiritually excitable. I orient my curiosity toward things external to me, and I use it, so far as is possible, in an objective manner. I never try to link my external experience with my internal, personal experience of myself, in the way that Lapthorn did. I perceived the wind as being within—I experienced the wind as though he were an independent part of my own self. Thus I acted toward the wind in a manner which was quite different from the normal spectrum of my reactions to things outside of me. I was *not* curious about the wind. I felt no compulsion upon me to even try to understand him.

But on Pharos, my relationship with the wind became a matter of vital necessity. It had been so, in a way, before. He had saved my life in the Halcyon Drift, and again on Chao Phrya, and perhaps on Rhapsody as well. But on those occasions, it had been a matter of an action which was as soon forgotten as it was over. On Pharos, I had to live with what he was doing for several days.

Like everyone else on Pharos, I was infected with the

killers which had been manufactured by the Pharos life-system. Unlike most people on Pharos, I remained quite unstricken by the viruses. While I am not by nature a violent man, I cannot claim to be free of aggressive tendencies, destructive impulses and anger, as some of the men apparently could. That I was not affected is not really to my credit but to the wind's.

The wind was merely a second mind sharing my brain and my body. But he was a far older mind, and a far more accomplished mind. He was able to make far more use of the mind-body identity than I.

In a way, he was more me than I was. But he was also discreet and valued a harmonious existence. He couldn't get rid of me any more than I could get rid of him, and he couldn't "take over" my body. He could walk while I was running, but all that would happen was that I would fall over—there was no question of one of us being able to overrule the other. What we did, we had to do together. The only areas in which he had total control were the areas in which I had none. The organization of the body against invading parasites was one such area.

He couldn't stop the actual invasion, and he couldn't kill the parasites once they were in, but he could and did efficiently combat the deleterious effects that they might perpetrate on my body. I wasn't immune to the Pharos bugs, but they couldn't kill me. That was good to know.

What was more, if anyone had a chance to figure out a viable combat strategy for use on a wide scale against the bugs, it was probably the wind. He might not have Markoff's know-how or Charlot's genius, but he didn't need microscopes to get in touch with the bugs. He could be that sensitive, if he tried.

How's it coming along? I asked him, on the morning of the fifth day.

—It's difficult, he replied. Refining consciousness to the molecular level isn't easy.

I thought it came naturally, I said.

—It does. When I'm free-living. But when I'm free-living I'm also practically dormant. You know how long it took me to get a purchase in your mind while we were both abandoned on that wretched rock. Reprogramming my genetic information into random patterns of air molecules didn't exactly leave me much self-consciousness to play with. Transferring my organization from one system of potential order to another may come naturally to me, but it doesn't entitle me to work miracles. You were an egg once, remember?

Not exactly, I said.

—Quite so.

Have you made any progress at all? I asked him.

—I've got a fairly good grasp on how the triggers are put together. We were right in thinking that the triggers were the things to look at—even though the viruses are different the trigger-mechanisms are basically similar. If we can deactivate one trigger, we can deactivate them all. And that's what we need, if we don't want the galaxy to be condemned to eternal peace—with humanity extinct as a probable side-effect. But getting the feel of the trigger isn't really enough. It's just not in me for me to perceive at that level what sort of an anti-agent, if any, could be effective against it. If Markoff can make a reasonable analogue of the molecule in his computer, I guess I can confirm whether it's accurate or not, so that the computer can work out an effective specific. But how long is it going to take to build an analogue? Months! *If* the computer has the storage space, which I doubt.

All in all, I said, you're getting nowhere.

—Well, he said, with what was almost an air of reluctance, not quite.

Go on.

—This is just my opinion, he said. And I can't guarantee its accuracy at this stage. But it seems to me that the trigger just isn't sophisticated enough to react in the way you think it does.

To specific chemical changes in the blood following strong emotional outbreaks.

—That's right. You've got to remember that such changes aren't all that specific. In terms of what happens chemically, one strong emotion is pretty much like another. The glandular reaction pattern is much the same for lust as for rage, for joy as for hate. In order for the trigger to be activated just by chemical balance in the blood, it would have to be coded to take account of a vast range of variables, and it still might not be one hundred percent reliable.

It seems to be pretty accurate, to date, I said. What alternative is there? Surely you're not going to try to pass off a telepathic virus on me?

—Not actually telepathic, he said. But something like. I think the stimuli that activate the triggers might be electrical. I think the viruses are sensitive to neuronic patterns.

Do you know of any other instances of that sort of sensitivity? I asked.

—Yes, he said. Me. And, if my assumptions are correct, the Pharos life-system. You see, that suggests a way that this mutation filtration system might work. Without natural selection, it's difficult to see how the life-system on Pharos manages to choose between alternative forms. There can't be any test of *viability* in the same sense that mutations on Earth are tested by circumstance according to their ability to survive. The only test the Pharos system can apply is one of pattern—life is order, and order has certain electrical patterns associated with it. It seems to me that the single crucial point in the evolution of life on Pharos—which may have been superficially similar to life on Earth at one point—was the evolution of this pattern-sensitive trigger molecule. The trigger promptly started turning Pharos into a perfectly ordered, perfectly stable Paradise. And the life-system's natural reaction to any invader or random mutation within itself is to apply the test-by-trigger. It was slow reacting to flesh of Terrestrial origin because of the differences in chemical composition, but the fact that it reacted at all at least implies that the system is electrically sensitive rather than chemically.

OK, I said. I'll buy it. So what?

—So instead of looking for something to chemically denature the trigger-proteins, try to find something to denature them electrically.

But at a molecular level, chemical activity *is* electrical activity, I said.

—Indeed, he replied, having anticipated the remark. But not necessarily vice versa.

I thought about it for a moment. What do you want us to do? I asked. Shoot five thousand volts through each other?

—Unnecessary, said the wind. Have you ever heard of echo currents?

Chapter 18

I took the brilliant idea to Charlot. He was pretty sick, but his mind was working fine. I told him the idea about the electrical nature of the Pharos mutational filter, and gave him a neat chain of hence and therefores leading him through the possible electrosensitivity of the triggers to the possibility of throwing the triggers out of kilter using magnets.

To be quite honest, I expected him to explode with laughter. It did sound a bit ridiculous, from my point of view. I didn't know what I was talking about, of course—the wind supplied me with all the patter. I just reeled it out. But it must have made some kind of sense, because it certainly fired Charlot's volatile imagination.

"It's a chance," he said. "A definite chance."

"There's one thing that worries me," I told him.

"What's that?"

"Messing about with triggers. Seems to me you'll have to be very careful. I mean, jerk it too hard, and the damn thing might go off."

He nodded. "We'll have to be careful, but that's only a minor point. If this is all correct, we have a way of attacking the viruses, and that's what matters. That's what we need—and quickly."

"Quickly?" I queried. "I thought the rush was all over. As long as we all stay peaceful, that is."

"You haven't thought this thing through," he said.

Not unnaturally, I was somewhat offended by that remark. "Haven't thought it through! My God, I've thought about nothing else. I've just brought you a complete diagnosis of the trouble. It might not be right, but my God, it represents some pretty solid thinking. And you

138

tell me I haven't thought things through. Had you worked out what I've just given you?"

"I would have," he said. "In time. But I'm not trying to minimize that. If you're right, you'll have contributed to a virtual miracle. And I hope you are right. What I meant about the time factor was that a ship from New Alexandria will be here in a matter of days."

"To help us," I said.

"If we can be helped. If not . . ."

"Then what?"

"You know perfectly well what these viruses could do to the people out there."

"So what? They're not going to do any harm while they're confined to the planet. We have all the time in the world to sort it out."

"And what about the Trisha Mellys of the galaxy?"

"Trisha? She's an idiot. But she's not dangerous."

"Oh, but she is. How many people do you think there are out there who would just *love* a chance to enforce peace on us all? How many men are there that would see these viruses as a gift from God rather than a possible disaster? How many men are there that would be infatuated with the idea of a Paradise such as we have here? What sort of demand do you think the whole Paradise Game is trying to satisfy?"

"But how could any man have that much confidence in himself?" I demanded. "Hell, I know we're all doing pretty well, but we're living in hope of a cure. If we thought we had this to put up with forever . . . How can any man be certain that he'll never again give way to anger, or hatred, or the impulse to strike someone?"

"Do you really want an answer to that?" asked Charlot.

"No," I said. "I get the drift."

"You see what I mean? We just couldn't afford to have a planet like this in the galaxy, unless we had a specific and definite way of counteracting the effects of its produce. I'm afraid that ship coming out from New Alexandria will be carrying a bigger responsibility than aiding us. Someone, somewhere, will take upon themselves the responsibility of ordering our destruction."

"The whole world?"

"The whole world."

"Nobody else knows about this?"

"Unless they've worked it out for themselves. It's not the sort of thing that anyone is going to talk about in the present predicament."

"You think they'd actually destroy us?"

"I'm sure of it."

"New Alexandria?"

"They're not the only ones involved. You know that. The galaxy is full of destructive people. Look at it from their point of view. Pharos is a matter of destroy or be destroyed. What other choice have they? We don't have time, Grainger. We don't have time at all. I don't know how long we have—how much they can afford to give us in their ultimate generosity—but I do know that if we can't cure this thing within their deadline, we won't be living out our lives in peace and harmony on Paradise. We'll be booked on a one-way trip into the sun."

"You're right," I said, feeling a little dazed. "You're quite right. I hadn't thought it through. Well, that being the case, I guess I'm doubly glad to have been of service in this little matter. I also think that perhaps I agree with Trisha Melly after all. I shouldn't have rejected her opinions out of hand like that. You're right—I hadn't thought the thing through. It honestly had not occurred to me that they couldn't even stand to let us live. *They!* Not Caradoc—not the out and out villains that nobody loves, but just *they*. New Alexandria and New Rome and the lot. You know, Titus, sometimes I think I'm stupid. Other times I think I might have been better off on that lousy lump of rock called Lapthorn's Grave."

"I'd be careful about getting too bitter and resentful," he said quietly. "It isn't healthy."

—Take note of that, said the wind. I can't work miracles. If you activate that trigger, we'll both have to take the consequences.

I sighed.

"OK," I said, "OK. I'll brood about it some other time. You go see Markoff, Titus. You start playing with that computer of his, and you see if you can come up with some magic magnetic remedy. Will we take it internally, do you think? Or will we just have to stand up to our necks in it? Anyhow, I wish you a speedy success, with all my heart. And can I please have a shot of something to make me happy? I feel a little fragile this morning."

"I'm sorry," he said.

"Coming from someone who apologizes about as much as I do, that's something," I said. "What for?"

"I shouldn't have told you."

"I'm bloody glad you did," I said. "If my friend and I had worked that one out between us, I might really have let the gun go off."

"Friend?" he queried.

"Figure of speech," I said. And I left him to it. I did get the shot, though. I really wasn't kidding about needing it.

Afterward, I went to talk to Johnny again, in the hope that it would cheer me up. It didn't. Despite the stimu-shot washing benevolence and strength of mind around in my veins, I found that the company of human beings made my mind contemplate nasty things.

It wasn't that I blamed anybody—certainly not. What Charlot said was quite true. The men who could destroy this world didn't dare not to, unless we found a way of defusing its artillery. Fair enough. You couldn't blame them. But on the other hand, it's things like that tend to make one cynical.

The worst thing of all, I think, was that I later came to the conclusion that the men who might—almost certainly would—have destroyed Pharos would have been wrong, in a way. The Pharos bugs wouldn't have destroyed the human race. We could have lived with them —and not just the one in ten or fifteen who never even got to stage two. After a while, even our guts might have stopped aching. We'd only have lost one in fifty right away—maybe one in ten in the final analysis. But even that runs to billions, I suppose. And there were only a lousy twelve hundred of us, plus a few thousand aliens. It all depends, I guess, on your economic theory.

Instead of talking to Johnny, I took a walk in Paradise. My attitude to it had changed. Before, I had reacted adversely to it. Now I had to wear a plastic suit to go out in it, and had to decontaminate myself every time I came home from it; it wasn't Paradise anymore. It wasn't even beautiful.

Beauty, as they say, is in the eye of the beholder.

I'd just inherited another blind spot.

I met some of the aliens while I was out walking. They approached me fearlessly, just as curious, just as playful as they had been the day the first Caradoc ship landed on their world. I let them walk with me for a while.

I liked them.

Chapter 19

By the time I got back to the ship, the sickness had filed a claim on one more body—Eve Lapthorn.

This meant that of the seventeen people currently resident aboard the *Hooded Swan* only three—one of the *Aegis* girls, Nick delArco (the original wouldn't-hurt-a-fly guy), and myself—remained unafflicted. That was a far, far better average than Caradoc was managing, however. They had about forty healthy people left to them— at least six of whom, it was strongly rumored, were the company whores. Markoff had been hit, and so had most of his staff, but they refused to lie down. They couldn't afford to stop working.

I called to see Eve the moment I found out the thing had dug its claws into her. She wasn't in bed—just resting, with an expression of valiant cheerfulness that looked as if it had been painted on.

"Hi," I said. "What did you do?"

"Nothing," she replied.

"That's what they all say," I informed her, with mock jocularity. "It came apart in me 'ands. Honest, it's a plant. I never touched the stuff. You have a sudden urge to beat somebody up?"

"No," she said. "If I got angry with anyone, it was with myself."

"Bit of a drag," I said, "when you can't even fall out with yourself in private without being called upon to suffer. This is Paradise all right. You are hereby ordered to be happy. Or else. It's a hard life."

"Sure is," she agreed.

"Is that really what happened?" I asked, striking a more serious note. "You got angry with yourself?"

"I honestly don't know," she said. "It could be that. But I think it's probably because I've slowly got to hating this place."

I nodded sympathetic understanding. "It's a difficult place to love," I admitted.

"You seem to manage," she said.

"I don't love it," I assured her. "But I slowly stopped hating it, instead of the other way around."

She gave me a long, steady look that made me feel a fraction uncomfortable.

"Just how is it," she said, "that an irascible bastard like you, who reckons to hate the whole damn universe, manages to hold this thing at arm's length, while the rest of us, one by one, let it into our systems?"

"I don't hate the whole universe," I said. "I just don't like it very much. I guess I just don't feel anything about it very much. Don't confuse me with Nick. He's holding this thing back with sheer goodness of heart. It's not getting to me because I haven't got a heart."

She was still looking at me.

"Your bark must be one hell of a lot worse than your bite," she said.

"Bite? I haven't got a bite. You know me—I'm too tiny to be a bother to anybody. I don't bite. I don't even bark, really. I just make noises."

She shook her head. "Nobody's too tiny to bite," she said. "What do you think is putting the bite on all of us, right now? It's the little things that bite the hardest."

I spread my hands wide. "In that case," I said, "I have no excuses. I don't bite because I don't bite. It's no use trying to work out why this thing hasn't laid me prostrate or kicked me right out like poor Ullman. That's the way it goes. I can't tell you my secret."

"It's a bit late now, anyhow," she said regretfully.

"Take it easy," I said.

"It *isn't* easy," she told me.

"I know," I said.

But she didn't believe that. She didn't see how I could know. She didn't know how I was surviving untouched by the Paradise bug, but she was sure that because I was, I couldn't understand. I think she resented the fact that she'd caught it but I hadn't. She'd been associating with the *Aegis* people—it was more or less inevitable that she'd pick up a little of their way of thinking. She saw this affair as a sort of testing ground—she thought that infection was a sign of weakness, of badness. A sort of stigma. I realized that she was jealous of me.

"They'll have the cure soon," I told her, but my voice was weak. Not because I didn't believe what I was saying—I was pretty sure they *would* have the cure soon. But because I knew it wasn't what she was thinking about. She thought that she ought to have been able to hold out.

It was a dangerous mood for her to be in.

"Look," I said, "I'll tell you why it hasn't got me. I've been cheating. I've been taking shots to keep my spirits floating. I had one earlier today—if I hadn't I'd be with you right now. If we'd thought there was any danger, we'd have given you shots too. But we thought you could hold out on your own. We had confidence in you."

Her eyes searched my face, looking for some traces of evidence that I was lying. I don't know what she expected to see.

"It would never have got Michael," she said levelly. I knew that was the core of the problem. That was the thought that was haunting her.

"It would have had him on the first day," I told her, and I wasn't saying it just to try to make her feel better. It was true. "Your brother was a great guy. He was as good a man as I've ever met. But he wasn't equipped for this sort of a fight. Your brother was brimming over with anger, just as he was brimming over with every other kind of emotion known to man. He couldn't have got by without it. He was what he was because he *reacted* to things, and his reactions were honest. He hadn't anything like the self-discipline that he would have needed to stay clear of this thing. It would have got him. Only stage one —just the aching gut and the runs, just to remind him, just to keep him in check. It wouldn't have killed him—

he didn't have that much aggression in him. But he was only human."

"And you're not?"

I was frightened by the bitterness that was obvious in her voice.

"Hell," I said. "I don't know. Maybe not. But Nick's human. And you're human. Nobody's going to start drawing any lines between you. Hell, *Johnny's* human. This bug doesn't mean a thing, in human terms. That's what we all keep forgetting. It's *alien,* is this thing. It comes from outside."

"It's objective," she said.

"It's *arbitrary,*" I corrected her. "This world is *not* Paradise—surely we've all realized that by now. It's not God's own heaven, set up to sort out the just from the unjust. That's not St. Peter's flaming sword that's nagging away at your gut. It's a *disease.* For God's sake, what does it *matter* whether your brother would have fallen ill here or not? He's *dead,* damn it. Neither of us is him. Neither of us *owes* anything to him. He didn't die because of me, and there's no need for you to try to be him because he did die. This is two years later. More than two years. We're on Pharos. It's nothing to *do* with him."

I needn't have gone on so long. The bitterness had already died in her. She knew that I was right.

"Shall I try to wheedle Charlot into giving you a shot?" I asked her. "We've got plenty, and that relief ship will probably bring a lot more. This tight rationing is only getting us into trouble."

"I'll be all right," she assured me.

"You'd better be," I said. "I'll never forgive you if you die."

And I meant that. I honestly don't know how much of the total conversation I had meant, but I certainly cared. The Paradise bug was making me care.

At this rate, I said to the wind, as we climbed back to the control room, I'll soon be caring enough to be hating this world along with the rest. You must be doing one hell of a job in there.

—Don't worry, he said. It's only a matter of time. I'm

sure now. Dead certain. It's the echo currents in the autonomic nervous system. It has to be. They have the right simple patterns. They're amenable to observation —the life-system would have had to learn the patterns that correlated with aggressive behavior, don't forget.

Learn? I queried.

—It didn't tailor this bug by intuition, he told me. Or telepathy. This life-system isn't sentient—just very highly organized. And very highly sensitive.

You aren't kidding, I said.

I settled myself into the cradle and I put the hood on. There was nothing I had to do at the control panel. I just wanted to get a look at the universe in its proper perspective. I get separation anxiety if I can't look through a hood once in a while to reassure myself that what my senses tell me is by no means the whole story.

I looked, almost reflexively, for the relief ship from New Alexandria, but she wasn't anywhere in the system. She wasn't due for a day or two yet. In any event, I decided, I wasn't mad keen on seeing her. If what Charlot said was true, medical supplies might not be the only kind of relief she was carrying.

I began checking through the stages in the call circuit. Merani was still manning the equipment at the camp, taking shifts with a couple of other men—the camp still had a relatively high proportion of healthy individuals. The mysterious Powell, whom I'd never seen, was still periodically involved at the town end, but he was ill. The town had decided that communications didn't have the priority to demand healthy personnel. The army still maintained a separate link in the circuit, despite the fact that it was only a hundred yards across the field. Military pride and protocol, I presumed. They, too, were using sick men to man that particular station.

There were no more deaths to report, and few more casualties. Everything had settled into an almost-equilibrium. We were used to the situation by now. Discipline in the army's ranks was, however, reported to be very slack indeed. After this, some said, this particular arm of the Caradoc organization would never function with military efficiency again. There was open conjecture as to whether the pacifists generated by the experience would revert to type the moment their guts stopped aching, and it was generally and cynically agreed that they probably would. But on the other hand, the consensus of opinion was that every man on Pharos would have been taught a permanent lesson in self-restraint and consideration, and that that in itself was sufficient to impair military psychology.

To a certain extent, that was a nice thought.

It led on, in fact, to lots of other nice thoughts. We had already considered what this disease could do to the galaxy if it got loose and went on the rampage. But there was a wholly different picture which emerged from the ideas about what this thing would mean to the galaxy if it could be harnessed and controlled. I didn't like to get too far ahead of events, but it did occur to me that these viruses were a great deal more valuable than the worms we had found in the caves of Rhapsody. They had great potential. Even my limited imagination was quite able to see that in the hands of New Alexandria and New Rome the Pharos viruses could change the face of civilization.

It was a bit of a pity, I thought, that if we did find a cure, and a way of controlling these things, that the Caradoc Company would have it too.

Chapter 20

The relief ship from New Alexandria arrived on the eighth day after the warning. It was not alone. Tracking it into the system was an armed ship from New Rome.

The newcomers weren't mad keen to be angels of mercy. They were apparently prepared to spend a good long while in orbit ascertaining the exact position on the ground. They wanted everything we knew and everything we thought, and to think about it themselves as well.

There was trouble almost from the first minute, when they were told that Charlot wouldn't talk to them himself and that Markoff could spare no one. Nick talked to them to begin with, having been briefed to a certain extent by Charlot, but Merani soon took over the main burden of reportage with occasional interjections from the other points on the open ground circuit. The men in the sky weren't happy about it, but several of the on-planet people were only too willing to tell them that if they wanted more details, then they were perfectly entitled to come down and have a look for themselves.

Eventually, after some hours of listening, talking, and thinking, several of them decided to do just that. They brought a boat down from the New Alexandrian ship. Once they were down, they wanted to see Charlot, and they weren't going to take "no" for an answer. Eventually, Nick and I had to lead them to Markoff's headquarters.

Everything therein was deathly quiet. Every time I had been in that particular copter previously the place had been a hive of activity—*everybody* had been doing something, not necessarily in a hurry, but in a way that suggested they were fully occupied and not to be interrupted. Not this time. All was still.

Markoff was sitting down, Charlot was reclining in one of the beds. There were not many other people in evidence, and those who were in the center of operations were obviously just waiting.

I didn't get a chance to exchange more than a few words with Charlot before I had to leave him to the relief team. But a few words sufficed.

"You've got it?" I said.

He nodded.

"How long before we know?"

"An hour."

"You tried it on yourself?" I asked.

He smiled—the first time I'd seen him smile in weeks. "Among others," he said. "I'm too old not to be expendable."

I knew that wasn't the reason. He thought he had a cure. When Titus Charlot thought he was right, he was willing to back himself. All the way.

The New Alexandrians took over, but he was in no mood to let them call the tune. These might be pretty big men on the Library world, but there was no one who outranked Charlot, and he wasn't about to cede any sort of authority to them in this matter. I stood around and listened to him while he browbeat them and threw the relevant information at them as if he were hurling spears. Watching him, I knew we were safe. He was in command of the situation. It would go the way he wanted it to go.

Well before the hour was up, the technical staff began to filter back and make ready for the crucial explorations. We were all herded out, then, while the medical staff got on with their job. We might just as well have gone back to the *Swan,* or even gone sightseeing, but we remained outside Markoff's copter, waiting.

We were joined by other men, alerted by the grapevine that affairs were coming to a head. After an hour or so had passed we were no longer a group but a crowd. By the time two hours had slipped by we were a very anxious and disturbed crowd. The doctors seemed to be in no hurry to put us out of our misery. There wasn't a man present who wasn't sick in his stomach at the thought that the supposed cure might not have worked. But we all continued to wait, constantly recharging ourselves with hope—hope that inside the copter they were merely sweeping away the last shreds of doubt—making absolutely certain that when someone appeared to give us the news it would be the goods.

We were well into the third hour, really feeling the heat of the sun through our clear plastic suits, when we were finally and irrevocably released from our misery. It was Markoff who made the announcement.

All he said was: "It works."

The crowd broke up just like that, and scattered. Everyone wanted to be first home with the news. Nobody but Nick and myself had come out from the *Hooded Swan,* and we both knew there was no point in making a race of it. We went back together, exchanging no words. We got into the airlock together, and when the inner door swung open, I waved him through. He was better equipped to deliver the release than I was.

It was me that had to tell them how, though. That was the task for which I was singularly well equipped, in that it was my mental parasite who had made the crucial suggestion. The *Aegis* people only wanted to know that everything was OK, but Just, Eve, and Johnny hung around while I showed off.

"It's quite simple," I assured them, "once you've thought of it. The viruses are initially carried into your body cells by bacteria. Once there, however, they invade cells in the gut lining, and ultimately establish themselves in nerve cells of the autonomic nervous system. The bacteria, of course, remained infected and potentially capable of infecting others, but they weren't any real problem to deal with, using ordinary antibiotic measures.

"The viruses, however, were more difficult. They existed in two forms—one, a dormant ring-form in the cytoplasm of the cell, caused no trouble at all. But when the ring-form broke and attached itself to the chromosomes in the nucleus, there was minor trouble caused by malfunctions of the autonomic nervous system. This happened in ninety percent of us. The symptoms weren't serious—just the sickness and general debility associated with minor infections. But this was only cocking the gun.

"The viruses also had a trigger which could make them subvert the entire energy of the cells, replicate themselves vastly, and reinfect millions of other cells throughout the body. We assumed to begin with that this trigger would be activated by chemical changes associated with aggressiveness and anger. But the glandular effects aren't the only physiological evidence of emotion—there's quite marked electrical activity in the brain. The mass currents in the brain are always confused with all sorts of other electrical activity, but the mentality of an organism isn't wholly confined to the brain and the central nervous system. For every gross change in the electrical activity of the brain, there is a distinct 'echo current' in the autonomic nervous system. It was a certain breed of echo current that was supposed to trigger the chromosomally-located virus, just as it was a certain breed of echo current that caused the ring-form to break, migrate to the nucleus and locate in the first place.

"This two-level activity was what initially offered the hope of a cure. The Pharos life-system as a whole has a far higher level of total organization than do Terrestrial-type life-systems, and its evolution at a molecular level has produced an extremely high level of electrical sensitivity about the molecular organizations employed in living tissue. Once Markoff had obtained a computer-model of the electrical patterns in the viruses—which was far easier than trying to build an absolute electrochemical model—it was only a matter of plotting the electrical interchanges which would take place between the viruses and various external charge-patterns. Echo currents can also be induced in the autonomic nervous system externally, by stimulating the hypothalamus, or even the inner ear. Eventually, Markoff and Charlot discovered a pattern which will not only deactivate the trigger but dismantle the virus. They can set up that pattern quite easily— they'll use the implanted electrodes in your case, Eve, and in mine. Other people will have to accept a little more discomfort, but they have the choice of electrode treatment and subsonic treatment.

"We've already done almost everything necessary to exterminate the bacteria that carry the viruses—once our insides are clean as well we can all go home. There'll be quarantine, of course, but it will only be a matter of a few weeks on a space station or on a dead world somewhere. The Caradoc people have agreed to abandon the world, and I think it's only a matter of time before New Rome proscribes it. They'll put a ship in orbit around it, to maintain a watch over the world, but that's all."

"Where do we start lining up?" Johnny wanted to know.

"It'll take time," I told him. "There's a lot of men with bellyaches down here. We can bring Merani's people back now, and the Caradoc people can start dismantling their town, provided that Holcomb and his excitable friend left them enough equipment to do it with. It'll be several days before everyone's been treated, and you can't expect to feel better instantaneously. But we'll be off this world in less than a week. All of us."

"What are they going to do with the virus?" asked Just. I had been talking quite long enough for him to get over the burst of elation which must have accompanied the news that he was going to live to enforce the law on some other innocent world. He was from New Rome, and while he wasn't the brightest peace officer I'd ever encountered he knew about the cold war that was brewing between the current aristocracy and the companies.

"I don't know," I told him. "Your guess is probably a lot better than mine."

"People are going to want to use this stuff," he said.

"Dead right," I agreed.

"On criminals," he said.

"And slaves," I said. "And political enemies. And on a lot of other people."

"It could solve a lot of problems."

"And create a lot more."

He turned away. I knew he had a lot of thinking to do.

But most of it would be personal. The ship that had come out from New Rome hadn't come for the ride.

I realized that it was time to start being frightened of Caradoc again. It was time to resume worrying about that battleship and the way it had spewed troops out all over the sky of a world where it had no business to be.

It was over—on Pharos. But it would continue, somewhere else.

Chapter 21

Quarantine was a welcome rest. It would have been far more welcome had we not had to share the facilities with twelve hundred Caradoc men. Mostly soldiers. But I did manage to join that card game, ultimately, and I didn't do too badly out of it.

The man who benefited most from the days with nothing to do but warm our backsides was Titus Charlot. It was probably the first time in years he'd taken a real rest, and it gave him a chance to recover as much as possible from the deterioration of his health which had afflicted him on Pharos long before we discovered the viruses. He would never be young again, that was sure, and he would probably never recover even the fitness and vitality that he'd had before we went to Pharos, but the period of quarantine set him up with a good chance of living a good few years yet.

I didn't see much of him, and he didn't seek out my company at any time either. He never bothered to thank me for the help that I'd given him on Pharos, and he certainly never thought of rewarding the devoted loyalty I'd shown with money or some relaxation in the terms of my contract. But I knew that it wasn't any use expecting miracles. He'd probably never been grateful to anyone for anything in his entire life.

One time that I did see him—briefly—he had some news for me. His eyes were glinting, and he had a distinct look of "I told you so" about him.

"You remember what we found on Rhapsody," he said.

"How could I forget?"

155

"We've duplicated the metabolic properties of the worms. In the labs on New Alexandria."

"Sure," I said, trying not to sound anything but resigned. "You told me that once people knew it existed they'd make it, if they couldn't have it made for them. You told me that it couldn't be suppressed. I know. Which city are you going to destroy to test the stuff?"

"None," he said.

"Things are really moving for you, aren't they?" I said. "A new ultimate weapon every month. By the time Caradoc decides on another confrontation, both of you will be able to destroy the whole damn universe in round one."

"I think that confrontation has been postponed for a while," he said.

"Why?"

"I think we proved something out on Pharos despite everything," he said. "We proved that the human race hasn't got the stranglehold on creation that Caradoc was ready to assume. There are more things to be dealt with than family squabbles."

"That doesn't sound like Caradoc thinking to me," I said.

"It is now," he assured me. "The war isn't quite what it used to be, now that our primary weapon is peace. Caradoc people are thinking things out. I believe that they'll come to the conclusion that greater subtlety is the order of the day. The naked confrontation policy they initiated on Pharos was a terrible failure."

"It sure as hell wasn't us who beat them," I pointed out. "That won't happen on the next world."

Charlot shook his head. "It would never have worked," he said. "Not on the scale Caradoc wanted. One world, maybe two. But it wasn't a policy for conquering a galaxy. That takes an awful lot more than naked force. Pharos was only one shot in the coming battle. But it's a shot they won't be trying again. There are different pieces on the board now."

"That's how you see it, is it?" I asked him. "Pieces on a board. A destroyer of cities and the meanest, most underhanded killer that nature's ever devised. That's all they are—two more pieces on the board. It's a game, is it? The whole of civilization just one big version of the Paradise Game?"

"You can look at it that way," Charlot said.

"*You* can," I said. "I'm not big enough to play games that rough. I couldn't even push the pieces. Hell, I'm nothing more than a pawn in the game myself. Your pawn."

"You could be a lot worse off," he told me.

"Yeah? In your hands I'm a king's pawn—how much more exposed can you get? I've almost grown accustomed to having people point guns at me, these last few months. It's becoming a reflex action to dive out of the way every time I see a flash of light. This isn't my idea of fun, Titus. It's not my kind of party, and you know it. I'm a simple man and I like a simple life. You know I don't like all these little affairs that you dabble your fingers in. You know I don't give a damn about playing the Paradise Game.

"You care," he said.

"Sure I care," I said. "I care who wins. But nobody wins anymore, and nobody ever will win. Every move we make, we get bigger and bigger pieces on the board. You're playing with forces that can sweep whole worlds aside, things that are bigger than a billion men. I know you're a genius, and I know you're always right, and I know that the Library has civilization in the palm of its hand, but the toys you're finding to play with are just too big. *They'll* decide the game, not you."

"So?" he said.

"So nothing," I said. "It's not my empire. I only work here."

"Grainger," he said, "men have been playing with forces that are bigger than they are ever since the Chinese invented gunpowder."

"So?" I flung his own comment back at him.

"So the practice has done us good," he said.

"It didn't do us much good on Pharos," I said, taking a new kind of pleasure in letting vindictiveness into my voice. "On Pharos, we lost. There's one Paradise that won't become a pawn in the game. And when it comes to the next planet, we won't be any better off because of what happened on Pharos."

Charlot shook his head. He seemed slightly amused. I knew that he was making a mockery of me, but I wasn't too upset about it. I didn't think he had the total understanding and the total control that he pretended. A king he might be, in his way, but I was pretty sure that history wouldn't give him the acclaim he expected, and wanted so badly.

But he had the last word on Pharos and the events associated with it.

"The Caradoc Company is playing the Paradise Game from the wrong angle," he said. "The primitive-Earth model of Paradise is no use. *That* Paradise Game was fought to a standstill a very long time ago. We *had* our unspoiled Earth once, you know. We had the primitive Garden of Eden. We lived in it. We played the Game to its conclusion then. We know the result. It was Paradise versus civilization.

"Paradise lost."

Brian Stableford
Halcyon Drift 50p

Out on the rim they said Grainger was the best pilot in the
galaxy . . . Starships were his life, and the *Hooded Swan* was
on her maiden voyage – a jointed articulated bird with
feathers of shining metal. Together they were hired for a
lethal race through cosmic storms in the dark nebula of the
Halcyon Drift, to find a legendary treasure-laden wreck.

'A breezily cynical hero and a planet with a creepy
metamorphic life-system'
BRIAN ALDISS, THE NEW REVIEW

Rhapsody in Black 50p

The trip to Rhapsody brought nothing but trouble. The
poverty-stricken fanatics who lived in its subterranean
labyrinths had found a source of riches – riches which could
destroy civilization. Grainger didn't fancy being alone in
the planet's black depths, pursued by outcasts and rebels,
even before he realized he had become Rhapsody's public
enemy number one . . .

Promised Land 60p

Starship Zodiac carried its cargo of men and women across
the centuries-wide interstellar gulf between Earth and
Chao Phrya and delivered its passengers into a Promised
Land. Into this hostile and mysterious world comes Grainger
aboard his starship *Hooded Swan* in pursuit of an alien girl
who could hold the key to the enigma of Chao Phyra . . .

Philip K. Dick
A Maze of Death 60p

Fourteen people arrive on the strange planet of Delmak-O,
each hoping to make a new start in life. . . . But there are
more endings than beginnings when murder claims one
victim after another . . .

In such bizarre situation the mounting suspense is matched
by an increasing surrealism.

Walter Tevis
The Man Who Fell To Earth 60p

Who was this tall, abnormally thin stranger who called
himself Newton? Why did he need half a billion dollars
immediately?
What was the secret behind Newton's revolutionary
inventions? Was there a master plan conceived in another
part of the Solar System?
Must Newton be destroyed by jealousy, mistrust and
suspicion, or can he save two worlds from destruction —
Earth and his own planet?
David Bowie stars in Nicolas Roeg's film of *The Man Who
Fell To Earth*, a recent successful British Lion release.

Theodore Sturgeon
Case and the Dreamer 60p

Three fantastic tales from the future and beyond
In Space . . . No one has been aboard the space ship for
over seven hundred years. It was designed for men like
Case, so they brought him back to life . . .
On Vexvelt . . . Why should human beings prefer to die
insane and in agony rather than accept the conventions of
this pastoral planet and its beautiful people?
On Earth . . . a dreadful, outrageous idea. But with money
no object the only way to know if something's impossible
is to try it.

You can buy these and other Pan books from booksellers and
newsagents; or direct from the following address:
Pan Books, Sales Office, Cavaye Place, London SW10 9PG
Send purchase price plus 20p for the first book and 10p for
each additional book, to allow for postage and packing
Prices quoted are applicable in UK

While every effort is made to keep prices low, it is sometimes
necessary to increase prices at short notice. Pan Books reserve
the right to show on covers new retail prices which may differ
from those advertised in the text or elsewhere